THE UNEXPECTED

STORY OF PURE SOUL

SONALI PATIL

Made with ♥ on the Notion Press Platform
www.notionpress.com

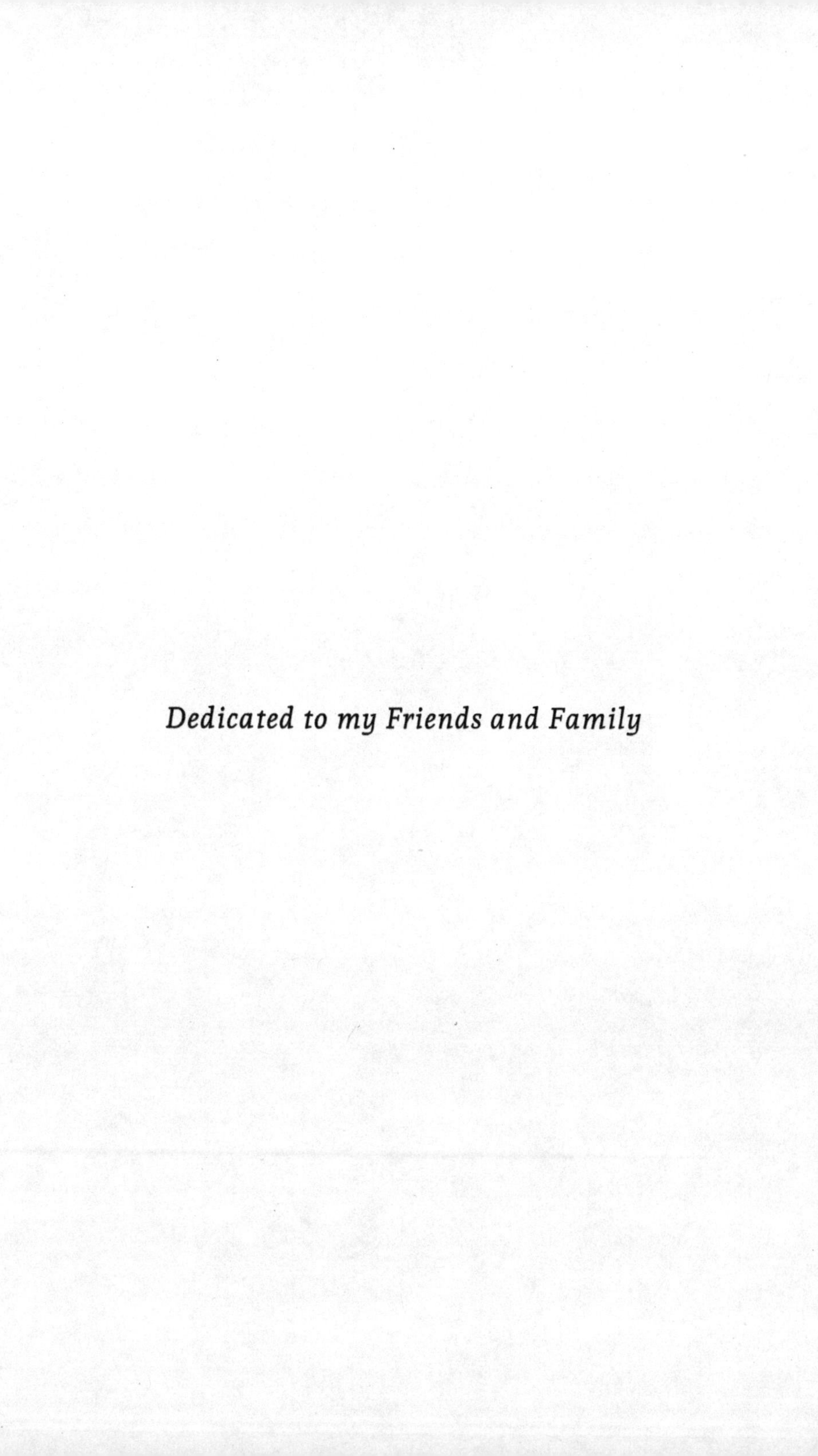

Dedicated to my Friends and Family

Contents

Foreword

Lost in my fictional world...

Preface

This is a fictional book with Love, Magic and Mystery...

Acknowledgements

Thank you to all my readers who inspired me to keep writing. You stuck with me through this whole time when my life was acting like a rollercoaster and being hard on me. I hope and wish this part of my life will be epic with all of you.

Love,

Yours Messy...

Sonali Patil

I

Good Girl

Sun was burning outside and Sana and Namratha were working on the project in Sana's room. Sana Patil was an arts student but she also had an interest in computers. She was a simple 21-year-old Indian girl from an educated family. She was a little chubby and 5'2 feet girl with medium and black hair. Namratha was Sana's best friend from school and she was a computer engineering student. She was a South Indian girl with having slim body, long hair, and big eyes wearing thick wing eyeliner.

'Sana I don't understand this code; where does it belong?' said irritated Namratha.

Sana didn't respond

'Sana this thing is confusing me, where should I put this?' said Namratha with more irritation.

Still, Sana didn't respond

'Sana, are you even listening to me?' Namratha Shouted.

After not getting a response she folded her laptop and pushed Sana's laptop to fold to see what Sana was doing.

She banged her hand on the table and shouted 'Are you kidding me? Sana wake up! why are you sleeping?'

Sana stumbled and woke up 'What happened?'

'What? I have to submit this project tomorrow and you are sleeping?' said irritated Namratha.

'I am sorry; I was working but I fell asleep' said Sana rubbing her eyes.

'Are you okay? Did you sleep last night or not?' asked Namratha with concern.

'No...' said Sana.

'Again that dream?' asked Namratha with concern.

Sana nodded. 'Yes!'

'Did you talk with your parents' asked Namratha.

'Yeah I did but they said it's just a dream so forget about it' said Sana.

'Ohh! So what are you going to do about it?' asked Namratha.

'Well... Nothing... right now we have to focus on the project and I am almost done with this and now we need to call Chaitali for this account stuff' said Sana.

ꟸ

'Hey, girls! How are you doing?' asked Chaitali.

She was a commerce student and excellent in accounts. She is also chubby like Sana with average Indian height. She has an elegant dressing sense. Her hair was long thick and black

'We are excellent but first tell me did you bring my Nachos?' said hungry Namratha.

'And my chocolates?' added Sana.

'At least ask me how I am?' said Chaitali.

'Ah...we don't need to ask you this you are looking beautiful...now please give me those Nachos' said Namratha twinkling her eyes like a kid.

Sana chuckled.

Chaitali sat on the chair in mischief dramatic way and said 'Listen to me ladies, I have sacrificed my precious afternoon sleep just to help you so you have to give me a lot of respect'

Sana chuckled softly and said in the same way 'I am so sorry for our misbehaviour your Highness; please forgive us and tell us how are you doing?'

And everyone busted with laughter.

And they started working.

'Sana did you guys fix the destination for the function' asked Chaitali

'Yah... At Alibag...they have booked a resort but I don't know its name' said Sana.

'Well I want to tell you something' said Chaitali.

'Remember you told us about your dream and that crystal thing' said Chaitali

'Yah! Did you find anything about it?' asked Sana.

'Yes! I guess I found something' She showed her mobile to Sana and asked 'Do they look like this?'

Sana nodded 'But what exactly are they?' she asked.

'These crystals normally get used in Witchcraft' said Chaitali.

'Sana is a witch?' asked Namratha.

'Shut up Namu... I am not' said Sana.

Namratha chuckled

'Does it mean something?' asked Sana.

'It means we have to complete our project that's it you old people' said Namratha.

Chaitali chuckled; gesturing to Sana 'No'.

ꕥ

Friday night Sana and her family reached Alibag. Everyone was so tired because of traveling they entered a resort that was booked for her cousin's engagement. The resort was so big and beside the beach. Everyone went to their rooms to get fresh so that all could gather for dinner.

Cousins had a special room to stay together. Everyone was meeting each other and cracking jokes. Sana was so happy to meet everyone. After getting ready all gathered at the dining area. Everyone was talking to each other and having dinner.

Guests from the boy's side were coming to Alibag on Saturday morning because of some reason; so they had more time to spend with each other. At one point, everyone realized that Uncle Rakesh was not there. Everyone started asking Aunt Sugandha about him.

She said he was quite busy on a phone call he would join us soon.

Accidentally the sauce in the bottle fell on Nisha (Bride) and her dress got dirty. She asked Sana to come with her to clean it. Sana was standing outside the wash room and Nisha was cleaning her dress. Sana was so tired that she was not even able to stand in one place she was searching for a bench to sit on. Meanwhile, she heard a familiar voice she went closer to that voice and she saw her uncle Rakesh was shouting at someone in a low voice on the phone. She was not able to hear she went closer to see what exactly happening. Uncle Rakesh was so frustrated and waiting for someone with one bag in his hand.

Suddenly one person came with another bag in his hand and he was asking Uncle Rakesh about some deal. Uncle Rakesh took out some jewelry from the bag and showed it to another man. Sana was not able to see the face of the other man because he was standing in the corner but when she saw jewelry..... it was a bride's jewelry and she understood that Uncle Rakesh was making a deal of this for something.

She shouted his name loudly and went to him to ask what was he doing his bag fell and she also saw some papers in that bag that another man had run away from.

"What were you doing Uncle Rakesh? Everyone is waiting for you at the dining area and you are here with this stuff?" asked Sana picking up the file and staring at Uncle.

Uncle Rakesh was quiet and staring at her with heavy breathing. She saw the file and she realized that the file was familiar too. She opened up the file and read and she realized that these papers are property papers of all family members. Sana lost her temper when she analysed the situation. She came to know that Uncle Rakesh was dealing with family property and the bride's jewelry without asking anyone.

She was shocked. "What the hell is wrong with you uncle? Have you lost your mind? What the hell were you doing?" she asked with anger. "Who the hell was that guy who was asking for this? What is happening?"

"Listen Sana beta," he said" You might have some misunderstanding I will clear it up, He was a lawyer and I was just checking the files if it was right or not"

"Shut up uncle," said Sana "I heard your conversation you were making a deal of something I know and you are lying to me are you even serious is this a time to check property papers? And what the hell that lawyer will do with this Jewelry? And if you are doing this then everyone should know about it, right? Then why the hell they are asking for you?"

Uncle Rakesh was shocked by her behaviour he said " You manner less girl is this way to talk with an elder person?"

She was staring at him and said "OK uncle I am sorry; I will tell everyone what happened and I will ask my doubts to other family members, bye!"

After listening to this he lost his temper and said "Don't you dare to do that you will have to pay for this mistake dear" with a curved smile.

She was scared and asked with gaps "What do you mean?"

"I will destroy you and your family "he whispered in her ear "What will happen to Bride if they break the marriage? How will she react? How will her family suffer? What if something happens with your parents" She looked at him sharply "Dear Sana every family member trusts me more than anyone how will they listen to you? They will never know who destroyed them so better way you shut your mouth and enjoy the function. You don't need to interrupt here I will take care of it"

"Why are you doing this?" asked Sana with gaps and staring at the way of the wash room wishing Nisha to come "They are your family"

Nisha came out from the wash room and searched for Sana. "What are you doing here alone? I told you to wait outside the wash room" said Nisha with irritation.

Sana narrowed her eyes *alone.* Searching with her eyes *where does he go?*

"Sana what the hell are you thinking about?" shouted irritated Nisha.

Sana shook her head and said" Nothing, what's wrong with you? Why are you so irritated?" getting back to normal.

"I have to change the dress, I am not able to clean this stain and it's looking so bad," said Nisha.

"Okay! Let's go to the room" replied Sana thinking about something else.

Is it the right time to inform someone about it? Everyone is happy I don't want to spoil anyone's mood but it is a very important thing I have to tell someone. What should I do? I have never seen Uncle Rakesh like this. What the hell is happening? Shit!! This is a mess! What if I inform someone after the function? But what if Uncle Rakesh did what they whispered in my ears?

Sana and Nisha went to the dining room to join everyone.

And suddenly....

"Hello my dear!!" said Uncle Rakesh to Sana with a fake expression of surprise and excitement to meet her. "It's been a long we met, but I didn't expect would meet like this" staring at her "She is the most innocent child in our family, and that's true" coming towards her.

He put his hand on her shoulder and said "I have never seen a girl like her innocent and brave" Everyone started looking at her with a smile and proud face. She was becoming uncomfortable with that situation.

She said with nervousness "Wha... What happened? Why are you all looking at me like this?"

"Sana I am very proud of you beta," said her father.

"But why? Dad I have done nothing "replied Sana.

"See I told you right! This is why I like this girl; she is not even showing off what she has done" said Uncle Rakesh loudly.

Sana looked at him sharply and said in a low voice "What are you talking about?"

"Sorry dear I could not stop myself from telling everyone what happened before"

Sana was staring at him she doubted that Uncle Rakesh must have lied something to family members.

"I told them about the thief you caught near the stairs, who was trying to run with all the jewelry" he continued

Sana was so shocked to listen to all of this. She raised her eyebrows looking at Uncle Rakesh with fear and anger. When she tried to speak uncle stopped her by holding her tightly. And whispered with a deep and scary voice "Did you see? I can do anything so don't you dare to forget my words".

Sana was so scared and her breath became heavier.

ஐ

The next morning, All guests started coming into the resort. Everyone was so excited, Sana was getting ready and thinking about not telling anybody anything right now. *I will tell Dad and Mom after a function.* She went to the Bride's room to help her get ready.

The bride and her cousin came to the ceremony hall from one side and the groom and his family members came from the other side. Sana was relaxed because she was going to tell her parents about last night so that she didn't need to fear anymore. Nisha and Mayank (groom) exchanged the rings and everyone started clapping.

All family members had choreographed some performances for the new couple. Uncle Rakesh came in front of Sana but she ignored him. Sana was also a part of the performance. After the performance everyone went for dinner it was a big hall with stalls of different food items.

During dinner, Sana was searching for her parents but she was not able to find them. She went to the room to check them, and she found her phone on the bed and she had 30 missed calls from her parents. She was trying to call them back but they were out of network. She came out of the room and she saw Nisha's mom and dad coming...

She ran towards them and asked them "Uncle, aunt did you see mom and dad? Where are they?"

“Relax Sana," said Aunt “They are in the hospital"

"WHAT" Sana was so shocked. She was so tense at that time "What happened? Why they are in the hospital? Where is the hospital? I want to go there" said Sana. She was so scared

"Sana relax they are fine, they went with Uncle Suraj and his wife," said Uncle.

Sana asked, "What happened to them?"

"Uncle Suraj was not feeling well, he fell from stares and got injured," said Uncle “Your Mom and dad gave us a message to tell you to stay here with us”

"Alright" replied Sana in worry.

After some time she got a call from her dad. "Hello!! Dad is everything alright?" asked Sana.

"Yes beta everything is OK," replied Dad.

“I was looking for you since dinner time, and when I came to my room I saw 30 missed calls from you, I was so scared Dad"

"I am sorry honey, we were calling you to inform you that we are going to the hospital with Uncle Suraj and then I realized about the rule we made to not to carry our cell phones in family functions," said Dad.

"It’s OK Dad", replied Sana “How is Uncle Suraj? And when you are going to come back? Where is the Hospital?"

"It’s a bit far from there beta, almost 60km. uncle’s leg got twisted when he fell from stares. He got scared so the doctor told us to stay here for tonight. Uncle is sleeping. We will come tomorrow, it’s too late beta now you go and sleep" said Dad.

"Yes Dad, you take care of yourself and Mom goodnight" replied Sana.

"Yes beta, good night," said Dad.

Sana felt too relaxed after talking with her parents. She experienced what real fear is...

ꕤ

The next morning everyone was packing their stuff and getting ready to go home. But all the cousins were planning to go for a hangout before leaving the place.

'Where are we going didi?' asked Sana.

'At Kolaba fort' said Nisha

'Ohh.. That's great' giggled Sana.

They booked a bus for Fort, everyone was enjoying it except Sana. She was thinking about her parent. She wanted to meet them and tell them everything about Uncle Rakesh.

All family members reached the fort and started clicking pitchers. Sana had a good knowledge of photography. She was also clicking photos. She wore a cute yellow top and three-front pants. Her hair was open. She was looking cute chubby little girl.

Uncle Rakesh offered her to click the pitcher of her and she ignored him. After some time Uncle Rakesh announced to gather everyone in one place.

He wanted to announce something. "I have a great surprise for all of you "

Everyone was looking at him.

"Who wants to go jet skiing?" he smiled looking at Sana.

All the cousins got excited and ran toward Uncle Rakesh to tell him that they wanted to do it.

"Okay then, I will pay for everyone let's get ready!!!!" said Uncle Rakesh.

Sana was silent she did not want to go jet skiing. She doesn't like water sports.

Nisha and Rahul came towards Sana to take her but she said "I don't like this. I am not coming, I have a fear of water, and you know I can't swim"

"No need to worry, can't you see their safety equipment its safe come on" forced Nisha.

"No!! I don't want" replied Sana.

"Sana come on my little sister we will have fun, OK I will sit with you for the ride is that OK? You will enjoy it Let go!!" said Rahul.

"But...."

"You are coming let's go," said Nisha with full energy and force.

Sana went with them and took her first ride with Rahul. And she enjoyed it a lot. It was a good experience for her. Everybody is done with one ride each.

"Do you guys want more rides?" asked Uncle Rakesh.

Everyone got more excited than before. Sana was also a bit excited She loved her last ride experience. But this time Uncle Rakesh gave some important work to Rahul so he was not available to go with Sana. Rahul suggested taking the assistant rider with her because everyone already left for the ride. And she agreed to it.

Sana was waiting for the Assistant rider to come for the ride. he took a bit of time to come and after a few seconds, Uncle Rakesh came out from the same tent. He looked at her and smiled at her. She saw him but did not react to anything and went for a ride. They went at full speed under the ocean in a straight way.

She was able to see everyone enjoying it and she was also enjoying after a few minutes She realized that she was not able to see anyone. She came so far from everyone. She asked that guy “Why have we come so far, the previous ride was shorter than this one"

That guy replied in a deep voice “Your uncle gave me more money for a big ride" with a slight smile.

“But where are others? Why we can’t see them? They are so far from us and I saw them returning from the same previous distance" said Sana. She was feeling more uncomfortable with the way they going.

‘Get me back to the beach’ said Sana.

He ignored it and continued riding.

‘Can’t you hear me? Take me Back to the beach’ she shouted with fear. He was sitting behind her. She moved behind and tapped on his shoulder telling the same. She was so scared that tears were coming out of her eyes. She bangs her hands on his hands but still, he ignores her. She realized that something was going wrong. She started screaming for help.

"Nobody can listen to you here," he said.

Sana started crying "Please take me back please! I beg you please, I do not like this Please take me back," said Sana with fear.

"Okay, answer my question first," that guy said.

Sana replied “What question?" he asked, "Can you swim?" Sana was stunned she was blank she was so scared and her gut feeling was telling her something bad was going to happen she was under so much stress. She was just staring at him with worry.

He smiled and pushed her into the ocean with full force.........

II

Where am I?

Sana was screaming for help. She fell but she was holding that boat...

She was begging but he did not listen.

he stood up 'You have to die my girl' he said looking at her.

'Please don't, I beg you' cried Sana.

'Goodbye....' whispered that guy and kicked her down.

She fell into the ocean. She was trying to float on the water but her hand was injured, she was trying but nothing was happening it was a time of low tide. She was not able to see land anywhere but the more she tried to go forward she was coming backward. She was tired a lot... she had no energy in her body. The climate was changing and Sana was feeling sick. Her vision started getting blurred..... she was not feeling any senses in her legs and arms. Her face was swollen and after some time she got unconscious.

ꝏ

'Where is Sana?' asked Sana's parents to everyone.

'Uhh... uncle we haven't seen her since we came back from the ride' said Nisha.

'What!!! , How you guys are so irresponsible? Where is my daughter? Go and find her' said her dad.

'Uncle we have been looking for her for 4 hours, She is not here we asked everyone about her nobody saw her' said Rahul

'What!, When? And how?' dramatically shouted Uncle Rakesh on the phone.

'What happened uncle?' asked Rahul.

'Sana did not come back from the ride, they are saying something has happened under the ocean they are not able to track the boat .... Which Sana was riding' said Uncle Rakesh.

Everyone was shocked....

'Nooooo .....' screamed Sana's mom. 'Why the hell did you force her to go there, I know she must have denied going there, she has a fear of water, why did you do that'. She was so scared and started crying 'I want my daughter back right now go and get her in front of me' She started yelling at everyone.

The whole family was scared after hearing what Uncle Rakesh said.

Everyone was searching for Sana for the whole day and night.

.

time passed....

"I think we should go to the police," said Rahul "We have been finding her since yesterday

Sana's father nodded.

After making an FIR police said "We will try our best to find her we will let you know all updates"

Sana's Family was in Shock so Rahul and his family decided to go with them to their house back

ꟷ

After a few days, the Sensei of Defence School in South Africa gets a call from local beachside fishermen

'Sensei! We have found a girl at the beach. She is unconscious and it looks like she is badly injured" said the fisherman

'I am coming' said Sensei.

(He is a 6 feet and dusky coloured person with 55 age wearing traditional clothes and a traditional cap on a bald head)

He went to the beach with some students and his son Cam. 'Where is she?' asked Sensei.

'She is inside the tent; Sensei, the doctor has come' said the fishermen.

Sana was lying on the bed unconsciously. She was very weak her body became so skinny and peeled white.

'How is she? Is she alright?' asked Sensei.

'She is so weak sir, it seems like she has not eaten since so many days been in the water for a long time.... She is having a high fever.... We have to do some tests and have to take her under observation so we can treat her correctly.' Said Doctor.

'But where is she from? How did she come here?' asked Cam.

(Cam is half Japanese guy... he is a five and half feet person with fair skin and small eyes with black hair.)

'We have to wait Cam; she is unconscious' replied Sensei

'But till then? What we are going to do? We don't even know her Dad, keeping her here can be dangerous, it can be a trap!' said Cam.

'Well; you are right son, but she is in very bad condition. Leaving someone like this is not in our ethics, we have to help her' said Sensei.

'But dad...' Cam was trying to say but Sensei stopped him and said 'It's my order'

'Okay Dad' said Cam in a low disappointed voice.

Cam did not agree with his father's decision he was worried about the safety of the school because his father had already suffered a lot in the past and the school was his home he lived there since he was a child.

.

Sana was shifted to the medical room under observation in the same school. Cam doubted her. He does not have trust in her so he decided to keep watch on her. All doctors were treating her with natural herbs.

It's been three weeks since they have been treating Sana.

After a few days, Sana started giving responses to medicines. She was healing; her body temperature was getting normal. She was mumbling something in unconsciousness nurse noticed that and called Doctor and Sensei.

'Mum...Dad...please help me, he will kill me...uncle...Noo.' mumbling Sana in a weak voice.

'It seems someone tried to attack her' Said the doctor.

Sensei nodded and asked 'Is she alright?'

'Yes, She will come to her senses soon, the way she is responding to medicine she will be fine soon, said the doctor.

'Good!' replied Sensei.

After two days Sana came to her senses and she opened her eyes. Everything was looking blurry to her. She was trying to wake up but she did not have that much energy. She was trying to call her mom and dad in a weak voice. She was not able to understand what was happening around her she was able to hear some voices but not able to understand anything everyone talking in a different accent. She got scared. She thought they were the same people who tried to kill her.

She asked 'Who are you? Where am I? What are you doing with me? Leave me I want to Go home' and she tried to come out of bed but she fell on the ground.... doctor and nurse tried to hold her but she refused help She screamed 'DON'T TOUCH ME' but she was not able to wake up.

The doctor was trying to handle her 'Don't be scared we are doctors, we are treating you, you are not strong enough to do anything girl you have weakness, trust us

Sana was listening but she was getting unconscious again.... She had a blackout in front of her eyes and fell...

After 4 hours she tried to open her eyes, and the nurse said 'You are so weak dear, don't be scared you are safe, no one is going to harm you, don't panic otherwise it will affect you' She was trying to make her comfortable 'relax, let me call doctor and Sensei'

Sana looked at her and nodded weakly.

After examination, Sensei asked 'Doctor, is she okay? Can we talk to her?'

'Yes Sensei you can!' the doctor replied

'Are you feeling good?' Sensei asked her.

Sana nodded weakly looking down at the floor she was feeling guilty about the way she had behaved before.

'What is your name?' asked Sensei

'Sana' she spoke in a weak voice

'Where are you from?'

'Panvel' said Sana in a weak voice.

Sensei narrowed his eyes and said 'Panvel? Where is it?'

'It is in Mumbai' She replied.

Everyone in that room was shocked,

'Mumbai? You mean Bombay in India?' asked Sensei

'Yes, right' with a confused expression 'Where am I? Which place is this?' she asked.

'Sana! you are in Cape Town, South Africa!' said Sensei

Sana was stunned after hearing that her eyes filled with tears 'How is it possible?' Sana was not able to believe that she had come this far from her family 'How many days I have been here?' she asked.

'It's been twenty-three days Sana' replied Doctor

Sana got so worried about her family, that she started crying. 'My mom and dad must be worried they must be suffering a lot. How they will come to know I am here in this situation

'I need to go Sensei, my parents must be so worried please help me, I don't know how to go back

'Sana you are so weak you can't go, you are not fit for travelling' said Doctor

'At least let me call them I have to inform them please' said Sana crying.

'We will inform them but first, tell us what happened with you. We need to know; you were mumbling something in unconsciousness; that seems something serious thing has happened to you, and also could be dangerous for you in the future' said Sensei.

Sana was looking at them she took a deep breath and said in a weak voice with tears in her eyes 'He tried to kill me....' She was not able to stop her tears and not able to speak a word.

There were only four members in the medical room nurse, a doctor, a Sensei, and a Sana

Sensei said, 'Sana whatever you tell us now will be the secret nobody is going to discuss it with anyone else. Is that clear?' he looked at everyone.

Everyone in the room nodded

Sana told them what happened at Alibag

'Oh my god, He is so dangerous' said the nurse

'No; He is evil' whispered Sana looking at the floor with moist eyes.

'So what do you think Sana if we inform your family about you; what your uncle will do?' asked Sensei.

'He will try to kill me again, and my family will be in danger too; He told me that if I do something he will destroy me and my family too'

Sana was so stressed she was breathing heavily. She was not feeling well she was becoming unconscious again.

ꟷ

It's been One month since Sana was missing, her family was suffering a lot they went to the police station every day but they received no information about her. One day they got news that the dead body of a girl had found Alibag at the same place. Sana's mom fell with tears her father was in shock.

Uncle Rakesh gave money to someone in the hospital to say that this was Sana's dead body. Her whole family was not able to believe in that situation. Sana's parents were stunned. They were broken. Uncle Rakesh managed the situation proving that it was an accident so that nobody could go to the police for further investigation and he would be safe.

Police told them that the body was decomposed we were not able to recognize her face but they can come and confirm if it is your daughter and claim the body.

Sana's parents went to the hospital to check the body. But the body was decomposed face was not recognizable her parents asked them for any other thing they found with the body.

Uncle Rakesh has already managed the things they gave them a necklace with the customized pendent of Sana which she used to love. He took that necklace from Sana's bag while water sports.

They gave that pendant to her family

Her family was broken; they had nothing to say and nothing to do. Their hopes were destroyed in a second.

Her parents said 'She is not dead; she is alive; our heart is saying that she is alive that body is not our daughter'

Uncle Rakesh said 'We have proof brother we have to claim that body otherwise we will not be able to do further rituals her soul will not get peace

They claim that the body came home they did all the rituals

Her relatives accepted that Sana was dead but her mom and dad did not accept; but for the formality, they did all the rituals.

ꙮ

Sana suddenly becomes unconscious.

'Stress is not good for her health right now it can affect her response to medicines' said the doctor

Sensei nodded he was thinking about something and worried.

'What Happen Sensei?' Asked doctor

'Did you notice something?' asked Sensei

'Yes Sensei I was about to tell you that'

Sensei looked at the doctor 'What?'

'Her recovery time; She has recovered so fast

'Really?' asked Sensei.

'Yes! I have seen her reports after this many injuries and pain a normal person cannot recover this fast; there were multiple fractures between her right wrist and elbow her shoulder was dislocated; She was unconscious for so many days and dehydrated when we found her on the beach. Her skin was damaged because of seawater; honestly I thought we would lose her but she survived.

But what you were talking about Sensei?' said Doctor

'We found her at the beach!' said Sensei

The doctor raised her eyebrows 'At the secret beach! Where only nominated fisherman can come'

'It's not safe to discuss it here, we need to talk with her but not now we will talk when she completely recovers' said Sensei

Doctor nodded.

ꕥ

After ten days Sana's Health was improving her digestive system was improving her fractures were healing faster and her injuries were healed. Her skin was looking healthier and her face was glowing. She just had weakness in her body.

Sensei sent his secret people to collect some information about Sana for safety. He came to know that everything that Sana told him ten days before was true. They found an FIR registered by Sana's family and also about the claimed body.

'Doctor; we need to talk! Take her to headquarters' said Sensei

Doctor and Sana took her to headquarters. It was a huge hall with a Japanese interior. A big but small height table was the there at center of the hall and one master computer on one wall. Sensei sat at one side of the table and Sana was in front of him. The doctor and nurse sat on the other two sides of the table.

'I need to tell you something Sana' said Sensei.

'What Sensei?' replied Sana.

'Your family has found your dead body and they have claimed that body' said Sensei

Sana raised her eyebrows and said 'WHAT... my body! But how? I am alive!'

'Exactly; that is a fake body; they claimed someone else's body as yours'

Sana was speechless and feeling broken inside but she asked in heavy throat 'Rituals?'

Sensei nodded 'Yes'

Sana remains silent with moist eyes

'I understand Sana how you are feeling but now you have to decide what you are going to do' Said Sensei.

'I don't know what to do Sensei. Now I don't even know the reason for being alive; I can't even go to my family I don't want to put them in danger because of me. I am dangerous for them' said Sana controlling her emotions.

'You have to decide it on your own Sana. There must be some reason otherwise why your destiny saved you?' said Sensei.

III

Truth and Lies

'I can't just sit and watch everything like a loser, I need to do something' whispered Sana.

Sana was so confused and stressed; she had no clue what to do next

'Would you like to be a part of our school?' suddenly asked Sensei

Sana remained stunned she asked 'Here?'

'Yes,' Sensei replied.

'But I don't even know which school is this, I don't understand what are you trying to tell me Sensei' said Sana

'I will explain you everything Sana' said Sensei.

'Sensei! What are you doing? How could we give her admission here?' asked the doctor in concern

'We will talk doctor' replied Sensei with an expressionless face

Doctor nodded

Sensei continued 'Sana this is a defense school and here we help student to find their relation with nature and with that relation, we help them to become good ninjas who are going to protect the world' and we call it Wingit.

Sana was surprised after listening to Sensei she asked 'You mean if I take admission here and take all training I will become a ninja?'

'No Sana we can't tell this right now it is dependent on your efforts and loyalty towards school' said Sensei.

Sana nodded softly,

'So think about it and tell us your decision' Sensei continued

'I will...' replied Sana suddenly

Everyone looked at her

'If there is hope, I don't want to lose any chance' she continued

Sensei looked at him gave a slight smile and said fixing his expression 'Tomorrow; your training will start girl'

'But She is not fully recovered Sensei!' said the doctor with concern

'She has no choice doctor, She has to start her training from tomorrow; only then we will be going to achieve what we want' said Sensei getting zoned out with his thoughts.

Doctor and Sana narrowed their eyes and looked at each other with confusion Sana gave a gesture to the doctor asking 'what is he talking about' and the doctor shook his head saying 'don't know' softly.

Doctor asked Sensei 'Sensei; What are you talking about? What do we want to achieve?'

Sensei got distracted from his thoughts and looked at Doctor sharply and said 'Don't you think you are doing more than your job doctor'

The doctor remains stunned after hearing such words from Sensei.

Sensei continued, 'Do you?'

Doctor shook his head and said 'I am sorry Sensei'

'Better' replied Sensei.

Sana was looking a bit tensed 'Wait; I want to know what do you want to achieve. Are you using me for your work?' she asked

Sensei fixed his face and looked at Sana, 'No dear; I am trying to help you. You are like my daughter and you are my responsibility. That is why your achievement is my achievement and I know your family is your achievement. That's all I want girl. I want you to be safe here; but I don't think you have trust in me dear, however, it's alright you can do whatever you want I was just trying to help you, if you don't want any help then....'

'I am so sorry Sensei, I misunderstood your words, I am so sorry; I will come to training tomorrow' said Sana in worry.

Sensei smiled and said 'Okay! See you tomorrow

Sana nodded and the doctor and nurse remained silent

'You may leave now' said Sensei.

Everyone nodded and left the room.

ℒ

After leaving the room Sana noticed that the doctor was worried about something 'Doctor! What happened? Why are you looking so worried?' she asked.

The doctor looked at her ignored and started walking again

Sana kept following him she again called him 'Doctor!'

After came out from the main building Doctor stopped walking and looked at her; Sana was following him so fast and she was tired of walking that much fast.

She again asked 'What happened doctor? Now I feel something is wrong, please tell me what happened

The doctor looked at her sharply and asked her in anger 'Who are you?'

Sana was looking at the doctor with fear inside her heart

'TELL ME; WHO ARE YOU' doctor asked with more anger

'Doctor! I am Sana' with gapes 'It's almost been a month you know me'

'I WANT TRUTH' said the doctor

'Doctor; I am Sana and I came from India accidentally; this is what all truth is' said Sana

'Then why Sensei is so interested in giving you admission here like this?' asked the doctor

'I don't know doctor; I had no clue about it' said Sana.

'I don't trust you; Sensei never talked to me like this, and today it happened because of you girl' said Doctor.

Sana remained stunned she had nothing to say

'Doctor please don't say this, I honestly have no clue why Sensei did that, but please trust me I am not lying about anything,

Whatever the truth is there in front of you' said Sana with gapes.

The doctor looked at her and said 'Nurse will show you your new room in school, now you don't need to stay in the hospital and leave the school

ഇ

It was her first day at school. She had no idea what she was going to learn. She entered the training area 15 minutes after the training time. She was wearing her pearl white uniform given by the school (the Pearl white uniform is for beginners who have not identified their spirit yet). She was looking for Sensei for further information about her training.

Cam was walking through the same path and when he saw her inside the school he lost his temper and went to her.

'What the hell are you doing here? How dare to enter our school?' said Cam controlling his anger and stepping closer to her.

She stepped back and said 'Sensei told me to come here, I am searching for him only'

Cam looked at her and said 'You liar'

'No.., no..no...listen to me I am not lying; you can ask Sensei' Sana replied instantly.

Cam grabbed her arm and pulled her to take her in front of Sensei

'Hey! Leave me it's hurting' said Sana while walking fast

Cam took her in front of Sensei and said 'Look Sensei I told you not to trust her, today she entered our school without permission, and she lied to me that you told her to come here

Sana looked at Sensei in pain

'Leave her cam' said Sensei

Cam left her arm and asked Sensei 'Now what Sensei, what are we going to do with her?'

'She is a student of our school Cam' said Sensei

Cam was shocked 'WHAT?'

'Yes, Cam! And I don't want any debate on this topic' said Sensei.

'But Sensei.....' Cam was trying to say something

'It's my order' Sensei continued looking at Cam in a deep voice.

Sana was observing the change happening in Sensei's personality but she shook her thought off and looked at Cam. He was looking disappointed with Sensei's decision.

Cam was a very nice person but he didn't want Sana to be in school for the safety of the school and his Father because of experience.

ꕤ

Sensei handover a book to Sana and said 'You have to read and understand this book it has all the rules, principles, and more information about our school'

Sana nodded 'Okay Sensei'

'Cam! Take her to a new class and introduce her to Blair'

Cam looked at Sensei nodded softly and left the office. Sana left as well to follow him.

It was a beautifully designed building with open ground students were practising and Blair was helping them train in defence and meditation.

'Hey Cam! How are you?' asked Blair when she saw Cam.

'Yeah I am fine' replied Cam with a disgusted face.

'However; here is your new student' continued Cam looking at Blair and pointing to Sana.

He looked at Sana and said 'She is Blair, She is going to train you; introduce yourself to her... I need to leave

Sana looked at Cam softly and nodded without saying anything. And Cam left the class.

'Hello ma'am I am Sana' said Sana looking at Blair.

'Hey come on don't call me ma'am you can call me Blair' said Blair with a smile

Blair was also an assistant professor at the school. She was wearing her Black uniform with sky blue coloured strips on her waist one horizontal strip on the right side and her blue batch on the left side. She is a 5 feet and fair girl with blond and long hair.

Sana nodded softly

'And I think we will know and understand each other while training so let's not waste the time and start training. But yes I will introduce you to other students' said Blair.

She continued 'Hey everyone pay attention, she is Sana your new classmate and I hope you will make a great bond with each other and help each other to grow

Everyone nodded and said 'Yes'

ꕥ

It's been 15 days Sana was practising her training regularly and finally, she got her 1st star of excellence. She was happy with the progress but also sad because she had no friend yet with whom she could share her happiness. Her classmates were not talking with her because of doubt. She was alone in a crowd. Suddenly Sensei entered the class. Everyone stood up in position and bowed down with respect.

'How is class going Blair?' asked Sensei

'It's going good Sensei; everyone is practising hard' replied Blair with a smile

'How is Sana doing?' asked Sensei

'She is a good student Sensei she is learning so fast and accurately' replied Blair

'Did you find her spirit? Which spirit does she have?' he asked desperately

'Sensei! It's just been 15 Days to her training; I mean not only Sana but no none of them found their spirits yet, they need some more time' replied Blair.

'I don't care about others I need you to find Sana's spirit as soon as possible' said Sensei in frustration.

'But Sensei it depends on her ability....' Said Blair but Sensei interrupted

'Start her further training soon and make her work overtime on it but do it it's an order you have to do that' said Sensei.

Blair was looking at Sensei, she nodded and Sensei left the class. Blair was shocked about Sensei's behaviour; he is a very calm person how could he behave like that and how could they don't care about other students; Blair was in deep thought and worried.

Sana came to Blair and asked 'Blair! Are you alright? You are looking worried'

'ah..yes.I am absolutely fine' replied Blair fixing her worried face

Sana realized something had happened she noticed Blair's worried face. It was the same way she noticed Cam and Doctor's faces while talking with Sensei.

ꕤ

It was a holiday Sana had no training so she decided to explore her school area by not going so far as per instructions given by Sensei

Sana was roaming in the area of the school

She noticed Sensei was going somewhere and he was in a hurry but he was hiding himself. Sana found it unusual. She spoke in her mind '*Why headmaster of such a big school need to hide like a thief*'

She decided to follow him. He was going a bit far from school but Sana kept following him

At a certain point, he stopped so Sana also stopped and hid behind the tree at a safe distance one lady came to meet Sensei (She was tall and thin, she had brown hair and white skin, and Big and sharp Gray eyes. She was wearing a black long dress with dark hoodie) and Sana heard their conversation.

Sana remained stunned after hearing everything she was not able to believe what she heard and saw there.

Sana's body was shaking with fear. She came back to school. She wanted to tell everything to someone what she looked

'*Oh my god! What is happening here, I have to tell this to someone but no one trusts me. Cam will not listen to anything he doesn't even want to see my face, the doctor also doubts me. What Should I supposed to do now? Who was that lady?*'

She sat on the bench. She was sweating with fear.

'*I cannot repeat the mistake I made last time. I have to do it on my own. I know that lady's name but who will tell me who is she.....yes!!*

Blair! She will give me the information

Sana ran towards Blair's Office. She knocked on the door and asked her, 'May I come in?'

Blair smiled and Said 'Hey Sana, please come in'

Sana entered and said, 'I am sorry to disturb you Blair; I know it's holiday but I wanted to ask you something

'Don't be sorry it's alright do you want something to drink juice or something you are looking exhausted' said Blair

'No thanks I just want bit water' replied Sana.

Blair gave her a glass of water Sana sat down on a chair and took a sip of water and relaxed

'So; what do you want to ask me Sana' Said Blair

Sana took one more sip of water and asked with a heavy heart but trying not to show any tension 'Yah... well. I want to ask that... Who is Martha?'

After listening to this Blair's face become faded, her breath getting heavier...

IV

Restricted Area

'Who told you this name', asked Blair with fear in her eyes and looking at Sana.

Sana observed Blair's face and she realized it was not a good time to tell her anything she realized one thing and she replied 'Blair, actually I heard some students were talking about me and mentioning me by that name; I mean I am Sana almost everyone knows my name but why do they call me Martha? Who is she?'

'Who called you by that name?' asked Blair.

'I don't know them Blair' replied Sana.

'It's okay Sana; don't take it seriously just ignore them' said Blair.

'It doesn't affect me Blair and I also know that it must be something bad otherwise they won't mention me by that name... but I want to know the truth; at least give me the idea' said Sana.

Blair was looking at Sana

'Blair please tell me! Don't you think I deserve it; if something is related to me I have to know about it right?' Sana continued.

Blair took a deep breath and said 'You are good with words Sana; okay I will tell you but in short, I won't tell you the whole story okay after that no questions alright?'

Sana nodded

Blair continued 'Martha was a very dangerous woman; she used to be a student of our school but she tried to harm our school. When

Sensei came to know about it they tried to stop her and a very big fight happened, many important people lost their lives, and the heads of our school decided to take her powers back; so after taking her powers back Sensei made a shield around our school so that she won't be able to come in...... but Sensei got stuck here.

Suddenly Sana asked, 'What? Got stuck? What are you talking about?'

'I told you Sana no more questions Now go to your room and take some rest and yes don't think about those people said Blair

Sana smiled softly and nodded

ꟸ

Sana went to her room... but she was feeling restless thinking about the same thing... she just couldn't stop thinking... she thought to take some fresh air so she decided to take a slow walk on the grass. Sana was walking on the grass and she saw two girls talking about Professor Lunes.

That was the same name she heard in conversation with Martha and Sensei. Martha was calling Sensei Lunes.

Sana went to those girls and said 'Hey! Ahh.. You were talking about Professor Lunes'

One girl replied 'Yes?'

'Can you tell me who is he? I mean which subject they teach?' asked Sana.

'Oh! He is a new Assistant professor, he teaches herbs and potions' Said the girl.

'Well; what is that? I never heard about it; I am new here and this subject sounds interesting can you tell me more about it if you don't mind?' Sana was a bit nervous but didn't want to show them so she gave giving fake smile to get more information.

'Sure! It helps us to connect with nature like medicinal herbs and everything, it says problem always comes with the solution we just need to find around it' said the girl

'Wow! Interesting! And potions?' asked Sana.

'These are like proper medicines which help us to survive in difficult situations there are some good potions as well as bad it is a very complex side of practical' said another girl.

'Where can I meet Professor Lunes?' asked Sana.

'We didn't see him for one month' said one girl.

'What!' Sana was shocked after hearing this

'It's almost been one and half years he has been teaching us but he never took any leave, he never missed any class but don't know what happened now' said another girl.

Sana was listening very carefully. And she replied 'It's alright I will meet him after he comes back' with a smile. 'Nice to meet you girls thank you for the information and your time she continued

Girls nodded with a smile and said 'Now we need to go will meet soon

Sana smiled and the girls left

Sana was standing in the same place in deep thought "What if everything *is connected? When I met Sensei for the first time he was such a kind person after that his behavior suddenly changed even I felt uncomfortable. He mates Martha ...to most dangerous women from whom he is protecting school....Martha called him Lunes but he is a professor in school who has not come to school for one month ... Does it mean Professor Lunes is Sensei? But why? And if he is here as Sensei then where is our Sensei....oh my god ....Martha!!.....what if she is planning to harm our school again...But why they were talking about me? Oh god, my brain is not working......"*

Sana was so worried... her body was shaking with fear she was having an extreme headache and she was getting weaker and suddenly she fell on the ground.

ꙮ

Sana was getting her senses back she opened her eyes and saw there were Blair, Cam, Doctor, and Sensei in the room. Sana was looking at everyone's face.

She asked, 'What happened to me?'

'We found you unconscious on the ground how are you feeling now?' said the doctor.

'I am fine doctor' said Sana with moist eyes.

'Are you sure? You are still looking weak and tensed' asked the doctor.

She wanted to talk about Sensei to him... she was about to say but she saw Sensei sitting next to her.

'Yes, I am fine, I was just missing my family a lot' replied Sana.

'She has to feel good doctor, now it is your responsibility to take care of her diet and medicines, and Blair you have to train her fast to make sure her physical fitness is good. Take care of her' said Sensei.

'Sensei! Why don't we give her a potion from Professor Lunes? How many days we are going to take care of her like a kid' said Cam.

Sensei suddenly shouted at him 'NO...We cannot give her any potion'

Everyone looked at Sensei with concern

Sensei continues by fixing his face 'She is our responsibility we have to take care of her... No more discussion do as I said and leave the room.

Everyone in the room was shocked.... Sana was looking at everyone's face.

'This is happening just because of you' said Cam pointing toward Sana with anger.

Sana's eyes filled with tears she wanted to tell everyone that he was not our Sensei but she couldn't because she knew no one was going to believe her. So she remained silent.

ꕥ

The next day Sana found near her pillow, it was the instructions of her diet and exercises she needed to follow for the next few weeks. Sana's head was still heavy. She was feeling so noisy there; she wanted to go to a silent place where her mind could get calm. And Blair entered her room 'How are you feeling Sana?' asked Blair

Sana looked at her and softly smiled and said 'I am fine Blair thank you'.

'Can I ask you something if you don't mind' asked Blair

'Yes of course!' replied Sana.

'What is bothering you? I can see and I can feel that you are in pain and tension; you can share with me we will help you with that' said Blair.

Sana looked at Blair with moist eyes she asked Blair with gaps and a heavy voice 'YOU TRUST ME?'

'Of course I do' replied Blair.

'But why? And how? No one trusts me in school who knows me, almost everyone thinks I am dangerous for this school; everyone thinks I am a fraud person how could you trust me?' asked Sana.

'Because I have seen you meditating Sana; I do understand people; I have observed you and examined you I know how pure soul you are and I have a gut feeling that I can trust you I can't see you suffering like this I want to help you

Sana became comfortable after listening to Blair's words...

Sana Said 'Blair! I cannot tell you everything but I want you to trust me whatever I will tell you

Blair nodded

'listen Blair; something has happened which is not good, I have seen something which I cannot tell you right now. But I think I can fix it; I am finding the way to fix it but I haven't found it yet. I promise you nothing will happen to the school. No one will get harmed, but I need to fix it before it gets worse, I need some silence to think about it. I need you to trust me on this Blair and please don't tell anyone about it I will tell you everything at the right time and place'

Blair was listening carefully and said 'Okay I won't tell this to anyone but promise me if you need any help you will tell me, we cannot take any risk about our school'

Sana nodded 'Promise' she replied.

After training Sana was taking a slow walk and thinking about the same. She came other side of the main building and she saw a church at some distance. She came to that side for the first time. She kept walking towards the church. When she reached she observed it was empty and old but beautiful architecture. It had 7 big marble pillars arranged in a circular direction with very fine crafting. She went inside and she felt peace. She looked around... but no one was there. She sat on the bench for some time with closed eyes...

There was a pin-drop silence but suddenly She heard a voice, 'What are you doing here?' the voice was very aged.. she opened her eyes and turned to her back.. an old man wearing an old beige coat was coming towards her...his face had a lot of wrinkles.. so does his visible area of hands too...

she stood up...

'What are you doing here young lady?' asked the old man.

'Actually... I saw this place from the main building so I came here to see it, it looks interesting' said Sana.

'No one stopped you?' asked the old man with his breaking voice.

'No! No one was there, but why would anyone stop me from coming here?... such a beautiful place is this' said Sana.

'Yes it is beautiful but it comes near a protection wall so not everyone is allowed to come here young lady...very few people come here' said the old man.

Sana remembered Blair's words she said about the protection wall.

'Protection wall which Sensei made right?' asked Sana

'Yes!' said old man

'It's good, isn't it? This protection wall will help to protect our school so Sensei can go anywhere without worry' she said knowing the truth...

'NO Young lady! Never think about it Sensei has sacrificed his whole life for this school. It's almost been 15 years since he didn't go anywhere he is the source of this protection wall' Said the old man.

Sana was listening very carefully *'If Sensei is the source of protection wall and that wall is still on... it means.....Sensei is in the school area only... He is not somewhere else...it means we can find him... but where?...* *She was lost in her deep thoughts...*

Within a moment she heard a voice and it broke her link... She looked around ...everywhere in the church that old man was not there he left the place without saying anything. But he left something for Sana...

There was a small pouch on the bench with a written note.

I hope you found your answers Sana; now don't waste your time and find him; open that pouch it will help you.

Sana was stunned... she took that pouch but she hesitated to open it thinking how did he know she was looking for something...but she did not want to lose any chance which would help her to find Sensei... she took a deep breath and opened that pouch and she found a crystal tied in the chain as a pendant and another note was written...

"It will show you a path....Use it if you need it"

.

Sana ran towards Blair's office.... she entered the office and looked at Blair with tensed eyes... 'NEED YOUR HELP... PLEASE COME WITH ME..' she said.

Sana took Blair to the place where she saw fake Sensei and Martha which is a bit far from school.

'Sana what happened tell me' said Blair in worry.

'We have to find Sensei' said Sana with a breaking voice.

'Sana! Sensei is already there in his Office I saw him going there' said Blair.

'HE IS NOT OUR Sensei!! HE IS FAKE.' said Sana with anger in her eyes.

Blair remained stunned 'Sana! Are you sure what are you talking about?' asked Blair.

'Yes! I know what I am talking about Blair, I saw Martha and that Fake Sensei together here; I heard their conversation, they were planning something dangerous... Blair we don't have much time we have to find him trust me please I will tell you every single thing after that I promise' said Sana.

'How we are going to find him' asked Blair

'Protection wall is still on right.... it means Sensei is here only, in school but we don't know where exactly he is.... And to find out I do have an idea about it.' said Sana.

'What Idea Sana?' asked Blair.

'Can we trace the power source?' asked Sana.

'We have so many power sources, Sana, many people are handling something on their own how will we find the exact one' asked Blair.

'Formula or type of protection wall..... It must be the same as Sensei's power, If Sensei formed that wall it means it belongs to them.... And if Sensei has not gone anywhere for 15 years so it must be the most powerful source, we can match them' said Sana.

'Sana! I don't know how to help you with this; do you have any other idea?' asked Blair

Sana looked at Blair and took a deep breath and said 'Can you connect with Sensei?'

Blair was looking at Sana and said, 'What are you talking about?'

'I read in our book about it; Students can connect with their professor with an inner connection like a telepathic connection' said Sana looking at Blair.

'I have never done this before Sana, how can I....' Blair was talking.

Sana interrupted 'Blair! You are looking so weak and tensed; look at your face'

'Yes Sana I am a bit tired' replied Blair.

'It's okay dear we will talk about it tomorrow you need rest' said Sana

Sana and Blair went to Blair's room Sana went into the kitchen and took warm milk for Blair.

'This is for you!! Drink it you will feel better' said Sana.

'Why it is yellow?' asked Blair.

'I added a bit of turmeric in this it will help you to heal fast and give you energy' said Sana with a smile.

Blair smiled and drank it. Sana took her to bed put a blanket on her and told her to take rest. Blair fell asleep. Sana waited for some time to make sure Blair was sleeping well. After confirmation, Sana went out of the room and locked her.

ꕥ

It was almost 11 at night and everyone was sleeping in school. Sana went to Blair's office and started finding the map of the school. (According to the book every professor must carry a map of the school for emergency use). Sana was found everywhere in the office. She suddenly heard a voice. It was Cam taking the last round of school for the day. She hid herself under the table. Cam saw that Blair's office's door lock was open he opened the door and saw everywhere he didn't see anyone so he closed the door and locked it. Sana was inside after Cam went she kept finding it. Finally, in one file she found it. She did not waste the time and started reading the map. She found some places where students are not allowed to go and some places where only Sensei can go. But she decided to find every restricted area.

Sana took out that pendant and looked at it 'I don't know how to use you but I trust you that you will help me and I will try my best' she said.

She wore that pendant and tried to come out of the office. The main door was locked so we went outside by the window. While opening and closing the window some noise happened. Cam heard that and came to see. He saw Sana running somewhere.

Cam got angry and said "I knew it she is not trustworthy" he decided to keep following her until she was caught red-handed.

She was checking the restricted areas one by one but she did not find anything it was 2 a.m.

But when she went near one of the south-restricted areas she found something weird happening with her pendant started.... It was shining abnormally the way she was getting closer to the gate it was acting weirder.

Sana's breathing was getting heavier and she was getting nervous but she continued walking.

She was surprised when she realized not a single security guard was there. She kept walking inside and Cam was following her at a safe distance.

She was scared it was too dark inside but the shine of the pendent was too much so she did not need any torch.

She Pushed the last huge and old door with her whole energy and opened it... as she entered she was shocked...

She saw Sensei and Blair...

They were tied up unconscious to the wall ....

V

Memories

Sana took a closer look at the room to see if anyone else was there or not. She didn't see anybody. She looked at the pendant and asked 'Can you heal people?' and the pendent started shining. She went into the room and looked at Sensei and Blair. Both were looking too weak. Without wasting time she went to them and tried to free them. Those ropes were very strong she was not able to open the knot so she ran outside the room and took Flambe to fire that rope. She fired that rope and tried her best to break it. After so much effort she finally succeeds. She took both of them on the floor. She was looking for water but didn't see anything.

Sana called them, 'Sensei! Blair! Are you okay? Please open your eyes... We have to leave this place as soon as possible

Both were too weak to say anything. Sana took out her pendant and tied Sensei's and Blair's hands together with it and she whispered 'Please heal them they need your help

And that stone in the pendant started shining again.

Cam was outside the restricted area he was waiting for the time when he would catch Sana red-handed

Sana was trying to speak with Sensei and Blair again and again. She was trying to wake them up because she couldn't leave anyone of them while taking anyone out of that area.

After a few minutes, both opened their eyes. Sana became happy to see them become conscious

'Sensei! Blair! Please try to wake up we have to leave this place said Sana

'We are trying Sana! But he gave us some kind of potion which is making us weak' replied Blair in a low voice.

Sana looked at the stone and said with an inner voice 'Please do something, please help them to heal

That stone again shined. Sana was telling them to focus on the energy they would fill but suddenly she heard a voice.

Someone banged the door too hard with anger. Sana became alert and said to that stone with an inner voice 'Protect them; make a shield around them and looked behind

A man was standing in front of her. He was looking so angry and said, 'You were not supposed to do this girl' with a deep and horror voice.

(He was 6 feet strong man with dark skin and deep honey-colored eyes wearing the clothes of Sensei)

'I know what I am doing....Professor Lunes' said Sana looking directly into his eyes with soft words and anger.

'I am giving you a chance girl, get out from here right now; you won't regret' said Professor Lunes.

Sana kept looking at him and said 'No I will not

She picked up that flambe and attacked him. She tried to bluer his vision with fire but he defended. He holed her hand and twisted so hard but she banged her head on his nose and attacked him again

Sana didn't want to hurt him so hard but she had no choice so kept she attacking him. She used all the techniques that she learned in the school and practiced. Professor Lunes was also attacking her and she was defending well but at one point she missed one attack and fell to the ground suddenly Professor Lunes picked her up and threw her on the wall so hard... she fell on the table. that table broke and Sana got injured She screamed in pain.

Cam heard that screaming voice and he ran inside.

Sana was trying to wake up pushing her hand against the floor but her back and one hand were seriously injured... She was not able to wake up.

Professor Lunes walked toward Sana and sat in front of her on his knees held her face and said 'I gave you a chance; girl; but you didn't listen to me now I have no choice I have to hurt you' with a deep voice and curved smile.

'Leave them ....' said Sana with gapes.

Professor Lunes got angry and he held Sana's neck tightly and lifted her.

Sana's eyes filled with tears because of pain. She was not able to breathe properly but still, she was trying so hard to be free.

When Cam entered in room he saw everything happening in the room Sensei shouted and said 'Save her'

Sana saw Cam and she suddenly got energy in her body and hope in her heart and lifted her leg and kicked Professor Lunes hard with all her energy and Cam attacked Professor Lunes as Sensei Said.

Sana got free and she started deep breathing. Cam was fighting with Professor Lunes..... Sana went to the Sensei and Blair to see how much they were healed. They got their senses back but the effect of the potion was still on.

Professor Lunes and Cam hit each other so hard that both of them were well-trained and strong so no one gave up... the point Cam fell and Professor Lunes took out the knife and attacked Cam but Sana came from behind and drove the pointed wooden part of the broken table in his leg and bang him with another wooden part exact between ear, neck and lower brain of Professor Lunes and he became unconscious.

It was 3 AM... Cam called security they arrested Professor Lunes. Sana told them about fake Blair sleeping in her room so they arrested her as well.

ജ

Sana, Cam, Blair, and Sensei everyone were shifted to the medical room. Doctors gave an antidote potion to Blair and Sensei... Medication to Sana and first aid to Cam.

'How did you find us?' asked Sensei to Sana.

'And how you come to know it's not us?' asked Blair to Sana exactly after Sensei.

'Do you want to know everything right now?' asked tried Sana.

'Yes! Each and everything' replied Sensei.

'Okay; I will tell you everything' said Sana and continued 'On the day of my admission I was getting weird feelings whenever I saw Sensei; it was feeling like he was a different person, he was not the same as I mate before. And not just me even Doctor, Blair, and Cam found your behaviour different than usual.... One day I saw that Sensei was going somewhere and he was hiding himself. I followed him and I saw he was with Martha and they were discussing something. I ran to Blair to find out who is Martha; she gave me a short intro of her is but at the end, she said something unknowingly that Sensei got stuck here then I started connecting every link'

'But how did you come to know about me? It was our last conversation' said Blair

'Yes It was our last conversation where I felt safe' replied Sana everyone was looking at her and she continued 'When I became unconscious; the next morning Blair came to me and started asking me questions and she said I trust you because she had seen me doing meditation very well' Sana smiled looking at Blair 'And only Blair knows that many times I used to sleep while meditation'

Blair chuckled

Sana continued 'I went to that building that looks like church for some silence... there I met an old man and he gave me this stone pendant with a note written it will help me to find you. I took that fake Blair to the same place where I saw Sensei and Martha I asked her to connect with Sensei but she didn't and she gave reasons'

Sana looked at Blair and said 'I saw you trying to connect with Sensei and I read it in the book after that I confirmed that she was not you so I took her to your room and told her to sleep'

'And she listened to you?' asked Cam

'No she didn't I gave her an Indian potion of sleep with milk so she had no choice, I can give you a guarantee that she will not wake up until tomorrow' said Sana with a soft smile.

'What did you give her?' asked Doctor

'I added whole Nutmeg powder in her glass of milk and gave her to drink' said Sana.

'You are smart Sana' said Doctor.

She smiled and said 'Thank you, after that, I went to Blair's office and started searching for a map of the school where I could find restricted areas. I went to every restricted area and after I reached where you were there that stone started acting weird and I found you both'

'Sana! You mentioned an old man; who was he?' asked Sensei.

'I don't know Sensei; I never saw him before' said Sana.

Sensei nodded 'Okay'

'But Cam! How did you come there?' Asked Blair

'Well... I was following Sana; I thought she was doing something wrong to our school but something else came out said Cam

Sana was looking at Cam in an obvious way

'Sensei! I think I should leave this School; I am not safe in this school and however, that fake Sensei gave me admission so it was not true or legal admission' Said Sana

'Of course! You don't even need to ask for this; please go. Are you waiting for the award for what you did today?' said Cam in a rude way.

'Cam, please! Will you stop behaving like this; I know you don't like me and I don't even want you to.... I was not talking with you okay I was talking with Sensei; you are not supposed to poke in between us' said a frustrated Sana.

'You don't need to say anything, just get out of here said Cam rudely

Sana was looking at him with moist eyes.

'And you know what you are a big problem of our school; you are dangerous for everyone' Cam continued.

After hearing all of this Sana broke down and her eyes filled with tears.

But Cam did not stop 'Your fake tears will not affect us girl; I have never seen an irresponsible girl like you; you don't even care about your family how could you do good with our school; you fake girl..... Shame on you; your family is so unlucky to have a girl like you

Sana lost her temper and shouted at him 'CAM...' with moist eyes.

'Don't you dare to call me Cam; my name is Cameron' Cam interrupted with a loud voice.

Sana took a deep breath controlling her anger and tears and said 'Cameron, please! Stop! Please don't say anything more it's hurting me

Cam shouted again 'Oh look; again new Drama'

Sana again lost her temper and said 'Shut up Cameron!'

Cam shouted more loudly 'You Shut up'

After watching all of this Sensei shouted more loudly saying 'I AM STILL ALIVE'

Sana and Cam both stopped fighting. Both of them have almost forgotten that they are in front of Sensei while fighting with each other. They looked at Sensei and nodded softly with guilt.

'I am very disappointed watching my students fighting with each other; I have never expected such kind of behaviour from my students' said Sensei.

'Students?' asked Doctor

'Yes! Cam is already our student; rather more than that but from today Sana is also our official student and because of bad behaviour they both are going to get punishment' said Sensei.

'Punishment?' Asked Cam.

'Yes! I will tell you the punishment after two days. Now go to your rooms and take rest' said Sensei.

Sana was trying to ask them something with fear she said 'But Sensei...'

And Sensei interrupted and said 'Apology for interrupting Sana but right now do as I said. He looked at everyone in the room and continued 'No more questions No more answers Go and take a rest

Everyone nodded and left the room

ꝏ

The next day Sana woke up so early. It was around 5:15 a.m. She was feeling fresh and healed. Her pain was almost gone after medication and rest. She was sitting on her bed and her eyes went to the pendent of Stone; on the small table near the bed. She picked up that pendent and started looking at it; she smiled softly and said 'Thank you for helping me now I should return you to your owner'

Sana came out of bed and got fresh; took that pendent put it in the same small bag and went to the church where she found that stone.

It was 6 AM and she reached church.

'Hello! Is anyone here?' Sana was calling that old man.

'I am here to return your thing.....Hello!'

Sana had been calling that Old man for so long but nobody responded.

She sat on the bench after a few minutes she heard the voice of steps; someone was coming inside.

He was the same old man she was looking for; she smiled and stood up

'It seems you are looking for someone young lady' said the Old man.

'I was looking for you sir' replied Sana with a soft smile.

'Why?' asked the Old man.

'I want to return this to you' She showed him the pouch in which she kept that pendent.

'I am sorry accidentally that chain of the pendant broke because of me and I don't know how to fix this' she continued.

The old man smiled and said 'You can keep this to yourself

Suddenly Sana reacted with a shaky voice 'NO...I am sorry I can't keep this with me; it's not safe with me; and I know I am not capable of this, you give this to someone strong and capable person; I don't want to create any problems again; I hope you understand

'Don't worry girl, I understand what you are trying to say, I will keep it safe and soon it will be there with its owner' said the old man and smiled.

'Well I want to ask you something, can I?' asked Sana.

'Sure!' replied the Old man.

'Who are you? And why did you help me?' asked Sana.

'You will come to know soon...' said the Old man.

He took that pouch from Sana and put his hand on Sana's head Sana closed her eyes for a second and when she opened her eyes that old man was not there.

ꕥ

The next day Sana and Cam came into Sensei's office together but they were not looking at each other.

'How are you feeling Sana?' asked Sensei.

'I am fine Sensei' replied Sana.

'So your Punishment will start from today' said Sensei

'How many days?' asked Cam.

'Until I tell you' replied Sensei.

'And what is the punishment?' asked Sana looking at Sensei.

'You have to work together, you have to go to the jungle or anywhere and collect wood for fire. Collect fresh fruits; simple and you are not allowed to take any vehicle. Everything should be manual'

'WHAT? TOGETHER?' said Cam loudly

'With him?' asked Sana in Shock.

'With her?' asked Cam.

Sensei nodded 'Yes'

'NOO...' Both said loudly.

'Well I am not asking you I am telling you said Sense

'Sensei please...' said Sana with a sad face.

'Okay then collect those wooden blocks or sticks at one place our volunteers will get them from there but don't forget to carry fresh fruits with you' said Sensei

Sana and Cam left the office and started walking toward the jungle

ꕥ

It's been 2 hours they are walking continuously

Sana was tired She asked Cam, 'Hey Cameron! How far is it?' with deep breathing.

But Cam ignored

'Hey please stop! I am tired' said Sana.

'Can you hear me, Cameron? I am tired can we take some rest?' said Sana again.

But again Cam ignored

Sana was exhausted She did not have that much practice of walking. At one point her Stamina broke and she Sat down to drink water, She thought she would follow Cam after a small break.

She drank some water took a deep breath and looked up and she found she lost the Cam. He was nowhere. She was near the forest but she didn't know about it. She kept walking following the path where she saw Cam for the last time and she kept calling him by his name 'Cameron'

After 10 minutes of walking, she entered the dark forest

'Cameron! Can you hear me? Cameron! Where are you' Sana was calling Cam.

The forest was very dark, confusing, and silent. She could only hear the noise of birds nothing else was there.

After some time she realized that she was lost in the forest. Her body started shaking. She sat on the big rock to relax but she saw a big hooded figure in front of her and she got more scared Sana was looking at the big hooded figure. It was a big and strong hooded figure wearing black traditional clothes and covering his face with black cloth.

'Who are you?; What are you doing here?' asked a hooded figure in a deep and scary voice.

'I am Sana, I came here with someone but I lost in this forest' said Sana with gaps

'With who?' asked the hooded figure.

'Cameron' Said Sana with gaps.

'And what if I found you are lying' asked Hooded figure.

'NO; I am not lying, it's true I came here with Cameron and now I am lost' said Sana with anger.

A hooded figure came closer to Sana; She got scared and tried to run away but that hooded figure caught her. He grabbed her hand very hard.

Sana was scared and she started screaming 'Leave me!' and began to struggle to free her hand

'Leave me; let me go'

While that her old same memory triggered her and she remembered the incident that happened with her in the sea during water sports and she broke down.

In anger, she pushed that hooded figure with all the energy she had, and that hooded figure fell. But Sana went zone out and she fell on her knees and started crying hard... she was missing her family so much.

Cam saw everything happened over there when he came back to find Sana. He never saw anyone in such pain. He was able to feel her pain by just watching her.

The hooded figure stood up and again came towards Sana to hit her but Cam ran towards him and stopped him.

That hooded figure was a security guard of the forest and he knew Cam for so long. So after talking with Cam, he went.

Sana was sitting behind the big tree and she was so scared and also she was still zoned out in memories.

Cam went to her and said carefully 'Sana! Are you okay?'

But she didn't hear anything

Cam patted her shoulder 'Sana look at me

Sana got distracted and panicked she shouted at him 'Leave me; don't touch me' with tears.

Cam was trying to relax her. He held both her hands quietly and said 'Sana relax it's me Cam you are safe; no one is going to hurt you; look at me; relax'

She came to her senses and started looking around

'What just happened....that hooded figure?' said Sana with moist eyes and gaps.

'He went away' said Cam

'When?' asked Sana.

'When you were crying and screaming' said Cam

Sana was so tired she was not able to understand anything.

'What! I was screaming?' asked Sana with concern.

'Yes, Sana! You were in pain; is something hurting you?' asked Cam with concern.

Sana was looking at Cam and said with a weak voice 'No...I ...I just.....remembered something' with gaps. She continues 'I am sorry; I shouldn't stop there....and....Do you have some water?'

Both of them took some rest and after feeling better both of them started to complete the task; they arranged wooded blocks and sticks together collected some fruits and left for school. After 3 hrs they reached school and went to Sensei.

'Have you completed the task?' asked Sensei

'Yes Sensei everything is completed' said Cam and Sana nodded.

'Good, now go to your room and take a rest; tomorrow you have to go again' said Sensei

Sana and Cam nodded and left the office without saying anything.

ꟿ

Cam was in his room and he was thinking about an incident that happened in the forest

'*Whatever I saw was real and true, I felt her pain it was too severe but what happened to her? I think I behave too harshly with her.*'

And Cam fell asleep.

The next morning Sana and Cam again came to Sensei's office and after that, they left for the jungle

While walking; 'How are you feeling now?' asked Cam

Sana looked at him with surprise 'I am good' she replied softly.

After one and half hours of walking, Cam said 'I think we should take some rest, Sana'

Sana looked at him and nodded. Cam offered an apple to her and said 'eat something you will get the energy

Sana was surprised to see this change in Cam's behaviour she took that apple and said 'Thanks Cameron' and smiled softly.

They started collecting wooden blocks and started arranging them.

They gathered some fruits on their way to their destination. After reaching the destination they took some rest and started working again. Cam was chopping large pieces of wood with an ax and Sana was arranging them and gathering the rest of the wooden pieces.

After finishing chopping Cam also started helping her gather them

But suddenly a snake appeared while picking up pieces of wood.

VI

You Matter!

It was Black Mamba. It is one of the most dangerous species in South Africa.

That snake was exactly as wooden colored and Cam did not notice it. But when he saw that snake it was already in his arm with wooden blocks. And within a fraction of a second, that snake bit him on the palm (Below the little finger on the palm).

Cam screamed with pain and threw all the blocks on the ground.

Sana heard Cam's voice she threw everything that she carried and ran toward Cam.

He had fallen on the ground.

'Cameron! What happens? Are you okay?' asked Sana in worry

The pain was extreme so Cam was not able to speak. But when he threw those blocks on the ground that snake got stuck between them. Cam pointed towards that snake and showed her his hand.

'Oh my god; did that bite you? Show me exactly where' asked Sana.

Cam was in pain which was unbearable

'Cameron relax; we will fix it; trust me just take a deep breath and don't sleep... Don't close your eyes; Show me' said Sana relaxing him.

Cam gave his hand to Sana's hand she saw that bit. She took a medium-sized rope from the bag and wrapped it around his arm very tightly.

Cam was getting weaker. Sana remembered a trick that her grandpa told her when she was a kid.

She shifted Cam to the safe side and started moving the blocks where that snake got stuck when she saw that snake she realized it was a Black Mamba and she needed to hurry because that snake is the most dangerous. She moved all the blocks carefully from that snake and started following it. She found a hole in which it entered exactly under one big tree. She collected some leaves from that tree and ran towards Cam.

'Cam eat them fast' said Sana.

Cam looked at her in shock.

'Cameron we don't have time to eat these leaves fast' said Sana.

She gave me some leaves for Cam to eat. Cam's hand was turning blue. Sana picked up a small knife from the bag and cut his hand where that snake bit was to flow out the blood with that venom.

'It's spreading fast. I should do something else.' said Sana with the inner voice.

'Cameron look at me; take a deep breath and don't sleep OK we will do something don't panic just relax and don't sleep' said Sana.

Sana ate remaining all leaves and gave one more cut to his hand. She took a deep breath and she started sucking the venom from his palm. Sucking and spitting out. She repeated around 7-8 times.

She looked at his hand; the color of his hand was getting normal. So she did that two more times.

Cam was getting unconscious but he was trying hard to stay awake.

Sana put some water in her mouth to gargle to take away the whole venom from her mouth. But accidentally she swallowed a few drops of it. When she realized it she again ran towards that medicinal tree and took more leaves.

She came to Cam and gave him to eat some more leaves. And she ate herself also she made a paste of some leaves and applied it on his hand and covered it with the same leaves.

Cam was feeling relaxed but he needed some medication.

'Cameron! Do you know if there is any hospital around here? We need to consult Doctor' said Sana.

'Go to east you will get help' said Cam pointing toward east.

'Is it so far?' asked Sana

'No' replied Cam in a weak voice.

'Okay stay here don't go anywhere else I will come back with help, and stay focused look here and there okay?' said Sana.

Cam softly nodded.

Sana ran towards the east as Cam said after ten minutes she saw some people working in the field. She was calling them loudly

'Hey! Please Help! We need help!' said Sana loudly.

Sana was also becoming weaker because of swallowed venom. But those leaves were helping her to stay awake and preventing her from venom.

After hearing this people in the field came towards Sana.

'Please we need your help; my friend got snake bit he needs medical help please help; we came here from Wingit the ninja school' said Sana.

'Wingit the ninja school?' asked one man.

'Yes!' replied Sana.

'Where is he now?' asked the man.

'Come with me I will show you" Said, Sana

Everyone started following Sana. Sana kept eating those leaves...

'There!' said Sana pointing towards Cam after reaching.

There were 5 men and 3 women with Sana.

'Cam! I found Help open your eyes' said Sana.

Cam was awake but not able to open his eyes.

'Take him' said one man from the group to other men.

They went to a small community established on a small piece of land

They took Cam into one hut for medication.

Sana was sitting outside the hut looking at the sunset but as the sun went down environment started getting colder. Sana was feeling warm inside and she started sweating she had no leaf remaining to eat.

After some time the heat started increasing in Sana's body.

One old man came out from the hut; he was a big and strong old man with dark skin and a long white beard. He was treating Cam. He came out and looked for Sana.

'How is he sir?' asked Sana.

'He is out of danger; rather he was already out of danger; you did a great job girl, you saved him' said the old man

'Are you sure he is totally fine? Nothing will happen to him right?' asked Sana

'Yes! Don't get stressed he is totally fine nothing will happen to him' said Old Man.

Sana was happy to hear that.

'But please don't leave him alone' said Sana in a low voice looking at the old man.

The old man nodded softly.

ꙮ

At 11 PM when the environment got colder Sana was able to feel more heat inside her which was painful and unbearable. Sana was sleeping in another hut.

She woke up to drink some water but she was not able to walk... her body started burning from inside.

She balanced herself by taking support from a pillar and called the lady sleeping in the same hut

'Hey!... Please help me; Ma'am! I am in pain please help me!' said Sana with gaps.

But that lady was in deep sleep so Sana made noise of vessels. After hearing that lady woke up to see what happened.

'Please help me!' said Sana with tears in her eyes.

'Hey what is happening with you?' asked the lady.

'My body is burning from the inside it's unbearable please call the doctor' said Sana with pain.

That lady went out from the hut to call that Old man

Sana was lying on the floor

'Hey Girl; what's wrong?' asked Old Man.

'My body is burning inside; it's painful' Said Sana.

'Did you eat something allergic?' asked Old Man.

'I ate those leaves wrapped around Cam's hand' said Sana.

'What? But Why?' asked the Old man in shock.

'While sucking out the venom from Cam's hand I accidentally swallowed a few drops of venom that is why I ate them' said Sana.

'What! Are you mad do you have any idea how dangerous it is?' said Old Man in anger.

'It's burning please help me' said Sana.

That Old man gave her one potion to drink. After drinking that Sana started vomiting.

She vomited around 2-3 hrs and she became weak but the burn in her body reduced.

The old man gave a paste to the lady and told her to apply it on her hand, leg, and stomach of Sana. As per the information lady applied that paste to Sana and covered it with a soft cotton cloth. And let her sleep.

ꙮ

The next morning Cam opened his eyes with blurry vision and an Old man was sitting in front of him.

'Where am I?' asked Cam to Old Man. Cam was unconscious when he had been taken to that place.

'You are in the Zulus tribe Cam' said the Old man.

'What!' said Cam with surprise.

'When you were unconscious your friend asked some people from our tribe for help' said the Old man.

Cam remembered he told Sana to go to the east for help. He softly nodded and said 'Thank you so much for helping us and thank you for saving my life

'No Cam! I did nothing; I only gave you medicine to heal fast. If you want to thank someone then thank your friend Sana. She saved your life by risking her own' said the Old man.

'What! I don't remember what happened that time; where is she? Is she alright?' asked shocked Cam.

'She is fine but under Observation, she accidentally swallowed a few drops of venom when she was taking it out from your hand' said the Old man.

Cam was looking at the Old man with shock.

'You are lucky to have a friend like her Cam; in this selfish world it's too hard to find pure sole like her' the Old man continued

Cam remains silent. He was looking at the floor with guilt about his behavior with Sana.

'I am sorry Sana.' Cam whispered to himself.

ꙮ

After some time few volunteers from Wingit the ninja school reached that place; where the Zulus tribe stays.

Cam was talking with other people in the tribe.

'Cam are you alright?' asked Herbert (leader of volunteers)

(He is a tall, fair, and strong guy with dark brown hair)

'Hey Herbert! I am fine but how did you find us?' replied Cam.

'I sent a message to your school yesterday night' said the Old man.

'Thank you' said Cam with a soft smile on his face.

'Where is that girl?' asked Herbert.

'Sana is sleeping in that hut' said Cam.

'Wake her up we need to go to school' said Herbert.

'Herbert! I think we should wait till she wakes up; she is so weak and she is unconscious' said Cam.

'We have a car; she can sleep in the car too' said Herbert.

'I think Cam is right; let her wake up on her own otherwise, we won't understand how much she has healed.

Herbert nodded and said 'Okay then we will wait

ꙮ

In the afternoon Sana was mumbling something.

'Mom, Dad please look at me.........Why are you not looking at me.....mom....dad.....I'm....I'm...

Al.....' She suddenly screamed 'NOOOO...' And she woke up stunned. She was breathing very heavy. And she started sweating a lot.

After hearing Sana's screaming Cam ran into her hut.

'Hey Sana; what happened? Are you okay?' asked Cam.

The old man came behind Cam.

Sana looked at Cam and said 'I am fine...it was...it was just a bad dream' with a soft voice and gaps.

'How are you feeling Sana?' asked the Old man.

'I am feeling good sir' said Sana soft voice.

'And Burn?' asked the Old man.

'It's gone' said Sana.

'Good! Now go and take a shower' said the Old man looking at Sana and turning to Cam and continued 'Now you can take her to school'.

Sana and Cam both nodded.

After some time Sana Cam and the volunteer left for school.

ꙮ

Sana had some weakness so she directly went into her room.

Cam went into Sensei's office.

'Son! Are you fine?' asked Sensei controlling his emotions and moist eyes.

'Yes Dad I am fine; fine, please don't worry' said Cam.

Sensei gave him a fight hug and said 'Take care

ꙮ

Next Day Sensei got a parcel which had Sana's name on it. So he called Sana in his office.

'Sana how are you feeling?' asked Sensei.

'I am fine Sensei' said Sana with a soft smile.

'I don't know how to thank you for saving Cam; yesterday he told me everything you did for him' said Sensei.

'Sensei please don't thank me just give me a blessing for my future that's it and let's not talk about it' said Sana.

'Okay! Well, Sana someone sent you this envelope' said Sensei.

'To me? But who?' asked surprised Sana.

'Don't know open it we may come to know' said Sensei.

'Okay..'

Sana opened that envelope and she was shocked after seeing this. Her eyes filled with tears and tears started running down from her eyes.

'Sana what happened?' asked Sensei

She gave that envelope to Sensei. He opened that and he also got a shock

It was Sana's funeral photos from India.

'I know who did this' said Sana with anger and tears in her eyes.

'Who?' asked Sensei.

'Martha....' Said Sana. 'I wanted to tell you something about that attack on you but that day you refused to talk about anything please let me tell you Sensei' Sana continued.

'Tell me now' said Sensei in a soft voice.

'Martha and Professor Lunes were planning something dangerous, and I heard that they want to use me for that; Sensei I think I am dangerous for this school and I should leave this school' said Sana.

'No Sana you are not going anywhere and nothing will happen to school we will protect our school' said Sensei.

'No Sensei please let me go; I will stay in your contact but please I can't stay here...since the day I came here so many things happened; I don't want to be the reason for anything, and I promise I will keep practicing everything and I think I don't belongs to this place or this place don't want to accept me' Said Sana with moist eyes.

'But Sana...' Sensei was telling her something but she interrupted

'Please Sensei; don't try to convince me please.' said Sana.

'Okay.... I won't force you to stay here but stay for two days I will arrange for you' said Sensei.

Sana was looking at Sensei.

'Just for two days Sana. Your safety is my responsibility' said Sensei.

Sana nodded and left the office with an envelope.

At the same time Cam entered in office he saw Sana going but she had tears in her eyes.

'What happened with her?' asked Cam.

'She is leaving the school Cam' said Sensei.

'What! But why? And you permitted her?' asked Shocked Cam.

'It's her decision Cam; She is in a very bad phase and I have to respect her feelings and decision' said Sensei.

Cam left the office suddenly and ran to Sana's room.

Sana was sitting in front of the window for sunlight and Cam knocked on the door.

'May I come in?' asked Cam.

'Cam! Yes please' said Sana and stood up.

'What happened?' asked Cam.

'What? Nothing has happened' said Sana fixing her face.

'Why are you leaving this school?' asked Cam.

Sana looked at him at said 'I have my reason, Cam'

'Then tell me we will fix the problem; Sensei will help us' said Cam.

'No Cam I just don't want to stay here; I don't care about anyone and I have no interest in living here' said Sana turning behind.

'Really you don't care about anyone?' asked Cam.

'None of your business Cam' said Sana in a rude voice.

'Where are you going to stay then?' asked Cam.

'I am not answerable to you Cam' said Sana.

'Okay fine at least tell me why did you save me? It's my right to know about it' said Cam.

'Nothing was special Cam it just because I was there if I hadn't been there, someone else would have' said Sana.

'But you would have died; you were almost dead' said Cam.

Sana looked at him but she had no words to say so she turned around.

'You had a choice, Sana. Why did you risk your own life to save mine?'

She remained silent.

'I saw your pain Sana; please say it Sana tell me your problem we will solve it; otherwise, it will kill you from inside' said Cam

Sana was controlling her emotions.

'Sana tell me why you risked your own life, Why did you save my life even though I treated you so badly?'

Sana broke down and started crying and said 'Because your life matters Cam and mine doesn't; your family must have waiting for you... but mine doesn't... Cameron'

She fell on her knees and cried. Cam sat down and held her and asked 'But why Sana'

'Because I am dead for them Cam; they performed my funeral and I can't go back otherwise my uncle will kill them' said Sana.

Cam was stunned. He picked up the pitchers lying on the ground and asked with gaps 'Is this your...?'

Sana nodded. She was not able to stop her tears, she wanted to scream but she couldn't...

Cam hugged her to make her feel safe. She hugged him back closed her eyes and cried for a long time.

After she calmed down Cam and Sana both sat on the floor and Sana told everything happened to her in the past.

Cam was feeling very guilty about how he behaved with Sana in the past.

'Thank you for understanding me Cameron' said Sana.

'You can call me Cam' said Cam with a soft smile.

Sana smiled back.

ഇ

After two days

Sensei arranged everything for Sana and Sana was leaving the school.

She took her bag. Sensei gave her some papers that she would need in the future.

'Sana take care of yourself and whenever you need any help just call me' said Sensei.

'Yes Sensei' said Sana.

Cam was there behind Sensei he was feeling bad that Sana was leaving the school.

Sana went towards Car and suddenly Sensei stopped her.

'Sana take this and always keep it close to you' said Sensei giving her that same pendent she returned to Old Man in church.

Sana nodded. She looked at everyone and at the end She looked at Cam.

And left the school...

VII

Time has Come

After 2 Months

'What? Are you serious?; this much happened in school and you didn't even inform us' said Daniel and Shawn.

(Daniel is a tall and fair guy with black hair and eyes and Shawn is 5.7 feet guy with dusky dark skin and black hair and eyes'

'Did you inform Terry about this?' asked Daniel.

'No... But he was with you at training; Where is he?' replied Blair.

'Oh... Yeah he got some extra work' replied Daniel.

'What work?' asked Blair looking at Daniel

'I don't know; Sensei gave him some work so he went somewhere, it must be confidential that is why he didn't tell us' said Daniel.

'By the way, where is that girl, Sana? We want to meet her" Said Shawn.

'She is not here; she left the school' said Herbert.

'Why?' asked surprised Daniel.

'I don't know she must have some personal reason' replied Herbert.

'Oh...Okay' Said Daniel.

'However, it's good that she's gone; she was so weird' said Herbert.

'What weird?' asked Shawn.

Everyone looked at Herbert with surprise

'Yah...Though she looks healthy she was always in the Hospital area. How could anyone be so delicate; if they know they are delicate then why the hell do they need to do all of these things; just to show off? ohh look how great I am' said Herbert with a rude gesture.

'Herbert! You are being judgemental' said Blair.

'No; I just said what I noticed.... And you know what I doubt that she made everything happen... didn't you notice that she was always present in that situation' said Herbert.

'Enough Herbert! Blair is right you are being judgmental' said Cam with little anger and guilt.

'Hey Cam....' Herbert was saying something but Cam interrupt

'Listen to me; I made the same mistake I judged her but now I am feeling guilty about it said Cam

'You don't need to be guilty Cam. She is no one; she doesn't even matter in our life' said Herbert.

Cam looked at Herbert he wanted to say something but he didn't

'Hey, man! Herbert! Listen; It seems very rude' said Daniel.

'Yeah exactly I feel the same' said Shawn.

'Okay fine....' said Herbert with irritation and continued 'Don't we have any other topic? We are just talking about Sana, Sana, Sana, Sana... we also have other things to talk about; can we talk about them? Let's ask them how was the training session. Can we?'

Blair chuckled softly and said 'Okay cool.. relax let's talk about something else, let's go to the canteen I am hungry we will talk over there' She looked at others and gestured them to relax and to keep calm.

ꕥ

Sana was living in Worcester. She was admitted to the academy to learn advanced coding and she was working in the small bakery of an old woman named Mrs. Oliver right below her apartment. The bakery business has been growing since Sana started working with that old woman because before that she was working alone with traditional method.

Mrs. Oliver was so happy because of Sana. Both of them made a beautiful bond.

One day Sana was coming with her new friend Terry to the bakery.

(He is 5.5 feet guy with dusky skin short black hair and black eyes)

'Why are you in such a hurry?' asked Terry.

'Today I have to help Mrs. O to complete some important orders; She will become more famous after that' said Sana.

'What important orders?' asked Terry.

'Yeah Someone gave us a very big order, we have to make a big customized Cake and so many cupcakes for the wedding' said Sana.

'Wow that sounds interesting, will you please get me one cupcake tomorrow?' said Terry.

Sana looked at Terry smiling and said 'Well. Okay I will give you 5'

Terry got excited and said 'What? Five...'

'Yes! But for that you have to help me with some work' said Sana with a soft mischievous smile.

'Ohh.. Business mind aah..' said Terry.

'Come on please Terry I need your help; I will be so busy after reaching the bakery' said Sana.

'Okay... Cool anything for 5 cupcakes made by you' said Terry (Chuckling)

'I will give you a list and money just get that stuff for me from the supermarket' said Sana.

'Okay cool; Deal yah..' said Terry and they both laughed.

ꕤ

'Hello Mrs. O I am back' said Sana with a smile after entering in bakery shop

'Hello Darling... Thank god you came on time we have so much work to do' said Mrs. O.

'Oh yes!' said Sana.

'Oh Hey Terry! You are also here; how are you my child and how are your classes going? And how Sana is doing in class?'

'I am absolutely fine Mrs. O; Classes are going so well, and our Sana is also doing well' said Terry with a smile and continued 'By the way you are looking younger day by day that is why many clients are getting attracted towards your Shop' said Terry with mischief smile.

"Shut up you naughty boy," said Mrs. O. and everyone started laughing including Mrs. O.

'Terry this is a list and money get this stuff okay' said Sana giving him a list.

'Yes Boss!' said Terry and went to the supermarket.

Sana and Mrs. Oliver chuckled.

Cam was reading every single book related to the moon and spells and rituals. And he found something so he ran toward Sensei.

'Dad school is in danger, Martha is going to use Sana after some days she is going to do something very bad' said Cam.

But Sensei was silent I deeply thought

'Dad, are you listening to me? School is in danger' Cam repeated.

'I know about this Cam' said Sensei with a soft voice.

'Then how could you be so silent and calm?' asked Cam

'Destiny is working Cam, we just need to be ready for a fight' said Sensei.

'What about students?' asked Cam.

'Will have to tell them the truth and let them leave the school for some days' said Sensei.

Cam nodded

'We have to announce it today itself' said Sensei.

'Okay Dad; but what about Sana? Who will tell her?' said Cam.

'Will see; first, tell students to gather on the main ground' Said Sensei.

'Okay' said Cam and left the school.

After finishing the order Sana and Mrs. Oliver sat at the counter to relax for a bit.

They were talking to each other and suddenly one woman entered a shop

She was tall and slim with Dark black hair and grey eyes in a red dress

Sana told Mrs. Oliver to take a rest and that she would attend to that lady.

'Hello, ma'am! How can I help you?' said Sana.

'I want one big and beautiful cake right now' said the lady with a rude voice.

Sana showed them all the cakes but the lady did not like any saying they were too small she wanted a big cake and she saw the biggest cake with Sana and Mrs. Oliver recently made.

'I want that biggest one; pack it right now" said the lady

'I am sorry ma'am that cake is already booked infect it was specially ordered cake I can't give it to you said Sana politely

Lady looked at her and said 'I will give to double that prize I want it right now"

'I am sorry ma'am! I... I Can't give it to you' said Sana.

Lady gave a curvy evil smile and walked towards Sana.

'You are Sana right?' asked the lady in a manipulative way

'Yah...' said Sana with gaps.

Lady went towards Sana and grabbed her arm tightly to hurt Sana.

'Umm...exactly as I heard about you....nice girl...true girl....but you are not looking strong enough' said the lady and banged her on the wall.

She was manipulating Sana.

Sana was afraid she looked into her eyes with moist eyes and asked 'Who are you?' with gaps.

'You didn't recognize me? Really?' said the lady.

'No...' said Sana

Lady banged Sana on the wall again and looked into her eyes. And said, “It’s me....”

Sana was looking into her eyes and the face of the lady suddenly changed.

Sana was stunned

‘Martha.....’ Sana whispered

Martha smiled like evil and said ‘That’s like my good girl

‘No...No...’ whispered Sana trying to get free...

Martha grabbed her throat and picked her up against the wall.

Mrs. Oliver shouted at Martha and Martha attacked her with her magic and she fell on the chair

Sana was getting hurt; she was trying to free herself looking at Mrs. O.

‘I told you right you are not strong enough; you have to be strong okay we don’t have much time’ said Martha.

Martha freed Sana and she fell to the ground. As she fell on the ground she ran to Mrs. Oliver.

Martha again went to Sana and weirdly looked at her Sana was so uncomfortable

She touched Sana’s face and body and whispered ‘Beautiful! I will take your beauty too... we will meet soon girl’

Sana stepped back and Martha walked out of the shop.

After a few moments, she again walked in and said ‘Well I don’t like NO’

And she destroyed that biggest cake with her magical wand.

ꟹ

‘Sana! My girl; are you okay?’ said Mrs Oliver.

Sana was about to cry but said ‘Yah I am fine. Are you okay? Did you hurt anywhere?’

‘No my child I am fine’ said Mrs Oliver.

Sana was sitting on the ground against a wall. She had a headache and she was so tense.

‘Sana! I think you should go home you need rest’ said Mrs Oliver.

‘No...I am going to make that cake again’ said Sana.

'You don't need to I will call that customer and tell them and will say sorry to him' said Mrs Oliver.

'No Mrs. O. I am not going to compromise with your reputation I will fix it and will go home, No more questions' said Sana.

ꕤ

Sana fixed everything and went home.

She was so uncomfortable she was feeling her wired touch again and again.

She took a bath 4 times but still, she was not feeling good.

She sat on the floor and her eyes were full of tears.

'What should I do? I can't even go anywhere she will find me. Not even in school otherwise she will directly attack...'

Sana was in stress she was suffocating inside. She wanted to cry and scream but nothing was happening.

She just sat against the wall staring at the other wall.

She took Cam's name to heart and talked to herself 'Cam please help me I don't know what to do?'

ꕤ

After the announcement, Cam was sitting in the office and he heard some voice calling him and talking with him

She looked here and there but no one was there.

He again heard a voice

'This is Sana's voice! She is asking for help but is this real or my mind is playing with me' said Cam to himself.

At the same moment, Sensei entered Cam's office room and said 'Cam you should leave for Worcester right now

'Worcester? But why?' asked Cam.

'To take Sana back to school' said Sensei.

'Sana is at Worcester?' asked Cam with surprise.

'Yes and she is in danger; Martha attacked her today' said Sensei.

'What?' said Cam.

He was thinking about the voice he heard a few moments ago.

'Don't waste time and go take your phone I will send you the location' said Sensei.

Cam nodded and left for Worcester.

ꙮ

At 11 PM Sana was sitting at the same place without eating anything. thinking about Martha and school.

'*What if I die before she uses me against school she will have no source to do anything. Something must be different in me that is why she chose me. If I die she will not be able to do anything*

Sana was in deep thought and she went to the terrace of the building. As she was feeling cold her thought to die was getting deeper. She stood on top and looked down and said. 'Now everything will be fine' She was about to jump but Cam grabbed her hand and pulled her down.

'What the hell you were doing? Have you gone mad?' Cam shouted with anger.

Sana looked at Cam and she became happy to see him she said 'Cam I found the way to stop Martha. She wants to use me but if I die how could she use me right? Everything will be sorted after that she will not be able to attack school or whatever she wants to do"

'Sana! Have you gone mad?... Are you out of your mind?' shouted Cam.

'No Cam it will work; think about it; let me go' said Sana walking towards the edge.

Cam again grabbed her hand slapped her hard and took her to the apartment.

Sana was silent and sitting on the chair. Cam gave her water to drink.

"I am sorry, I shouldn't have slapped you.' said Cam with guilt.

'Cam listen to me it will work' mumbled Sana.

Cam held her hands and said 'Sana look at me; whatever you were doing was a temporary solution. If you die she will find someone else the difference is it will happen after a few days, and then you tell me how many people will die for school?'

Sana looked at Cam with moist eyes.

'Sana I can understand your concern towards school but we have to fight with her; running away is not an option; we are not cowards' said Cam.

Sana looked at him realizing her mistake 'I am sorry Cam; I am so stupid. Thank god you came otherwise.....' said Sana breathing sharply. 'But how did you come here? And how did you find me' asked Sana.

'Sensei sent me here; he came to know about the attack Martha did on you' said Cam.

'She didn't attack me! I mean she did but she did not come to attack me; She came to see me' said Sana looking at Cam.

'What? What are you saying?' asked Cam.

'Yes, Cam! She attacked me because she got angry with me; I didn't listen to her; and she was so weird Cam! I didn't like it, it was disgusting; she was sounding like she wanted me my soul my body my everything' said Sana.

Cam noticed Sana was being uncomfortable with something...

'What did she do to you?.. Why are you so uncomfortable Sana?' he asked with concern.

Sana took a pause... 'She disgustingly touched me... I didn't like it Cam' said Sana.

Cam was feeling angry and bad about it.. but he was more frustrated because he couldn't do anything about it...

'Did she say something to you?' asked Cam.

'Yah' said Sana she continued 'she said I am not looking strong enough; I have to become strong, we don't have much time"

'Time for what?' asked Cam.

'I don't know what exactly she is going to do' said Sana.

He wanted to make Sana comfortable so he decided to change the topic to make her feel better..

.

'Okay! Well I am so hungry do you have something in the kitchen to eat' said Cam.

'Oh! I am so sorry I didn't even ask you for water, but I cooked nothing today I was not feeling to eat anything' said embarrassed Sana. 'Just give me 10 minutes I will make something for you' continued Sana.

'Well great! It means you also ate nothing; you sit I will make something' said Cam and went to the kitchen.

Sana followed him but Cam told her to sit down on the chair so she sat. Cam found bread and some other stuff so he made a roasted sandwich and cold coffee for both.

He took everything on the table and said 'Dinner is ready this is a hot roasted sandwich and cold coffee to make your mood light'

Sana chuckled and said 'this is so embarrassing for me'

'Oh come on don't be embarrassed I will also give you a chance to cook for me now eat this' said Cam.

They both laughed

'Sana I think you should come to school with me; Sensei sent me here to take you back to school you will be safe there' said Sana.

'But what if Martha came to school and hurt other students' asked Sana

'She won't hurt any student we sent everyone to back their home for some days' said Cam.

'Okay then I will come with you; by the way, dinner was tasty' said Sana.

Cam chuckled.

ꕥ

Sana wrote a letter to Mrs. O and Terry that she was leaving the apartment and she would meet them soon and slide it under their doors.

Sana and Cam left for School.

It was 5 AM and they had almost reached school.

But suddenly something came in front of the Car and they met with an accident.

Cam and Sana both were fine they only got some scratches on their body.

They came out of the car.

'Cam! Are you okay?' asked worried Sana.

'Yeah I am fine are you okay?' asked Cam.

'Yes, I am fine.... But what was that?'

'I don't know Sana. I don't see anything here' said Cam looking everywhere.

He looked at Car and said 'This never happened with Car'

'What?' asked Sana.

'This Car is one of the strongest cars but look at the damage now; this is weird' said Cam.

'Cam I think we should leave this place; I am not feeling good' said Sana.

'Yeah me too... school is not so far from here we will walk to school let's go' said Cam.

And they started walking towards school.

But suddenly someone attacked them with a blast and they both fell.

They woke up and saw a lady standing in front of him with some people with covered faces.

And Sana whispered 'Martha....'

VIII

I Accept You

Cam looked at Sana and said 'get ready to fight

Sana nodded

Martha attacked them.

Sana and Cam fought hard. Cam was happy to see Sana fighting like a warrior they made all covered face people injured. Everyone was on the ground.

Martha swung her wand and more people appeared and she shouted 'Catch her

Cam began to protect her and he fought with every single who was trying to touch Sana.

And Sana was fighting too.

Sana saw that Martha attacked Cam with her wand.

Sana shouted 'Nooo...don't you dare to hurt him

She ran to Cam lying on the ground. He got up and they both attacked Martha but Martha again attacked him with her wand. Cam fell on the ground very hard and was getting unconscious. Those people grabbed Sana; she again started fighting with them.

After realizing that her people can't stop Sana, Martha attacks Sana with her wand.

Sana fell to the ground but she was less injured than Cam. Those people came to Sana and grabbed her again and took her to Martha.

Sana was trying so hard to get free she was calling Cam loudly. Cam was trying to get up but he wasn't able to Sana was shouting 'Leave me please; leave me....Martha, you are not doing this good....Leave me'

Cam was able to hear Sana's voice but his vision was getting blurry and suddenly everyone disappeared

ꕤ

Cam opened his eyes in the hospital. Sensei was sitting next to him. Blair, Shawn, Daniel, Herbert, and Terry were waiting outside the room.

'Dad!' Cam whispered.

Sensei looked at Cam and smiled with a drop of tears in their eyes 'Cam; are you okay son?'

'Yes Dad I am fine but she took Sana; I could not save her Dad, I am sorry' said Cam with a low voice.

'It's alright Son I know you tried your best, and we will find her and save her nothing will happen to her' said Sensei.

Cam nodded.

ꕤ

Martha took Sana to an unknown place and she was locked in the dark room.

She was knocking loudly on the door and trying to open the door. One of her legs was tied with an iron chain.

"MARTHA.....Leave me...you are doing wrong" shouted Sana.

But nobody replied. Sana sat down against the wall. And after some time she fell asleep.

After some time someone entered that dark room; she heard footsteps and woke up.

'Who's there?' asked Sana. But no one replied footstep was getting closer to her

'Who's there?' she asked again.

Suddenly someone grabbed her hair tightly and spoke in a deep horrifying voice 'You make so much noise..I don't like noise.. if you do that again I will kill you"

Sana got scared. But she said in anger 'Who are you; leave my hair"

'Shut your mouth otherwise, I will have to cover your mouth with a bandage' said the shadowed figure.

'No... I will not; tell me who are you and where am I' shouted Sana with anger.

That shadowed figure got angry and slapped Sana so hard that she fell on the floor and became unconscious.

ഇ

It's been 2 days Sana was unconscious and she had no idea about it because that room had no window to understand anything if it was morning or night.

When Sana came to her senses she found herself tied up with Chains and rope. Her hands were tied back. Both legs were tied with strong rope and her mouth was covered with bandage. She tried to get free but nothing happened

Cam and his whole team were trying to track Sana but no one found her in 2 days.

Everyone was finding her in different places

'We have to find her soon; we don't have much time we have only 4 days after the super moon we won't be able to save her" said Blair to everyone

(It was November 2016 when the Moon was going to come very close to Earth. This happens once in 69 years. And that time many powers get stronger)

Sana was tied up with ropes and chains in that dark room and she was not able to do anything. She was hungry she had not eaten anything for 3 days so her stomach was making a 'ghrrrrr....ghreeeee' kind of noise.

Sana was speaking to herself 'Cam.... I am sorry I couldn't stop her'

Cam was in headquarters and he again heard the same voice he heard last time and he recognized it. He sat and started to concentrate on the voice and replied 'Sana! Is that you?'

Sana was sitting with closed eyes and she also heard the voice of Cam. She thought it was Cam she started looking here and there and started making noise but no one replied.

Cam again asked her with an inner voice 'Sana! Can you hear me?'

Sana again heard something she said 'Yes I can but where are you? I can't see you"

Cam said 'Sana try to concentrate on your inner voice; we all are trying to find you but we don't know where you are please tell me where are you"

Sana understood that she was getting connected with Cam directly through an inner voice, she concentrated and said 'Cam! I don't know where I am; she has locked me in a dark room I can't see anything"

Cam replied 'Sana try to give me any kind of clue, any voice any smell anything you can feel'

Sana said 'No cam I can't hear anything this room has no window it is just a dark block'

'Sana you have to do something; we need to find you.... check every corner of the room' said Cam.

'Cam I can't they have tied me with chains I can't even move' Sana replied

After listening to this Cam got worried.

'Are you okay?' asked Cam.

Sana just replied with 'hmm'

'Don't worry Sana; you are strong we will find you soon just keep giving me updates tell me anything you see, hear anything' said Cam

'Okay' replied Sana.

And she again tried to get free from those chains.

That shadowed figure again banged the door opened it and shouted 'STOP MAKING NOISE YOU BLOODY GIRL'

Sana was not able to speak anything because her mouth was covered with a bandage. But her stomach was still making noise.

He got angry again he went to Sana grabbed her neck and picked her up.

Sana was getting hurt, she was not able to breathe and trying to get free but suddenly Martha entered the room and she lit up the room. And she saw that the man was trying to kill Sana. Martha took out her wand and attacked that man and he died on the spot. Sana fell hard on the floor.

She looked at that man and she got so scared that her voice not coming out. He had no skin on his face. He was looking so horrible.

Martha went to Sana and opened the chains. Sana's body was shaking with fear.

'Get up and come with me' said Martha.

Sana looked at Martha and her tears started coming out Sana said with pain in her heart in a very soft voice 'Why Martha? Why....'

Martha grabbed her hand and took her to another room.

It was a beautiful room decorated with different curtains, a big soft bed with soft pillows, and a big wardrobe full of clothes and accessories.

'Go and get fresh baby; and wear whatever you like from wardrobe it's all yours, and yes you must be hungry I will arrange some food for you' Said Martha looking into the eyes of Sana.

Sana was not able to understand what was happening but she still nodded softly.

While coming into this room Sana heard the voice of ocean waves.

Sana went into the bathroom and concentrated on her inner voice 'Cam! I heard the voice of ocean waves.'

Cam listened to that and replied 'Great Sana! You did a great job. Now listen to me don't make any fight with Martha. Just listen to her whatever she is telling you she won't hurt you for the next 2 days because she needs you just keep updating me'

Sana replied 'Alright' and went to get fresh.

Cam told everyone 'Don't find her in the city; we need to cover the ocean sides'

'What? But how do you know that' asked Shawn.

'We don't have time to explain; I will tell you everything after all of this' said Cam.

Everyone nodded and started covering every ocean side.

ᘓ

Sana took a good hot bath and wore a beautiful and simple peach-colored dress.

She was looking like a beautiful angel.

Martha entered the room with a lot of food; she looked at Sana and smiled like an evil.

She walked towards Sana... Sana stepped back but her back touched the wall behind her..

Martha came closer to her... and touched her face with the tip of her finger... Sana was getting uncomfortable... 'Such a pretty face and such a soft skin..' she whispered.

Sana was scared looking at her.. trying to avoid her touch..

'Eat whatever you want and sleep you will feel better' whispered Martha again

Sana looked at her and just nodded.

Martha left the room and locked it.

As Martha left Sana felt relaxed she took a deep breath.

She was feeling hungry so she ate some food...

After eating food Sana was feeling better and more powerful but also she had sleep in her eyes.

Sana went to bed to relax her body.

After some time she heard a big noise of something and she woke up 'It sounds like a siren' she thought.

She got closer to the window and started looking everywhere she didn't see anything but she was able to hear some noise.

She closed her eyes and tried to contact Cam "Cam! I can hear something but I don't know what exactly it is"

It was 4 a.m. and Cam was in headquarters with Shawn and Daniel. But they both fall asleep. He heard Sana's voice 'What noise Sana?' he asked.

'I don't know cam it has mixed with waves noise I can't hear it properly' said Sana.

'Sana concentrate you can do that; please do it' said Cam.

'Okay,' Sana replied and concentrated on the noise. She said 'It's kind of siren'

'What siren?' asked Cam.

'kind of factory siren may be' Said Sana.

'Sana gives me some more details' said Cam.

'They are announcing something in between' said Sana.

'But what Sana..' shouted Cam.

Sana's eyes filled with tears she said with gaps 'I don't know Cam....' She sat down on the floor.

Cam understood how Sana was feeling he was feeling guilty because of his harsh behavior

'I am sorry Sana I didn't want to hurt you' said Cam.

'No Cam; it's not because of you I am feeling helpless right now' said Sana sobbing.

'Sana trust yourself; even if we don't come you have to fight' said Cam.

'But Cam she is so powerful...' said Sana.

'You are more powerful Sana, you have a pure soul, and my Mom told me a pure soul can do anything; and I know you can' said Cam.

She nodded and meant while she heard something

'Cam! They are repeating one word again and again' said Sana.

Cam took a deep breath and said 'What word Sana?'

'something like kob....kobee....kobeer' said Sana.

Cam's eyes started shining he asked 'Sana is that Koeberg?'

'yes..' replied Sana instantly.

Cam found the map of that place.

'Great Sana! I knew you can do it; we are coming' said Cam happily.

'Guys wake up we found Sana' Said Cam to Daniel and Shawn.

'What? Where?' asked Daniel.

'West coast, she is near Koeberg nuclear power station' said Cam.

'Great! Let's go to Sensei' said Shawn.

'Yah; I will call everyone' said Daniel.

'Okay let's go' said Cam.

ꟗ

'Are you sure Cam that she is there?' asked Sensei.

Everyone gathered in the office. It was '5 AM'

'Yes Dad I am sure' said Cam.

'How far is that?' asked Sensei.

"30 kilometers from here we will reach in an hour," said Cam

'But do you know exactly where she is?' asked Blair.

'No Blair, but we can find her surely she is not in that power station she is in the ocean' said Cam.

'What?' asked Herbert.

'Yes! She was just able to hear some noise in those waves which means she is not that far from the station' said Cam.

'Listen I don't know how you find her but it could be a trap; because no one of us found her only you did' said Herbert.

'Herbert has a point Cam' said Sensei.

'I am sure it is not a trap trust me' said Cam.

'So how we are gonna go?' asked Daniel.

Cam smiled

'I will need Daniel, Blair, and Terry with me to find Sana. And Herbert, Shawn to cover us after finding her Terry and I will go to her, and Blair and Daniel will meet you guys and if we need any help we will contact you' said Cam.

Everyone nodded and left to find Sana.

ꟗ

Sana was feeling good because they were coming to help her but deep down she was worried too.

Sana was sitting on the chair thinking about Cam's words.

Martha came into the room and sat in front of Sana looking into her eyes.

Martha smiled slightly. She took her wand and waved towards Sana. Her gown was automatically changed. Her peach gown turned lime color and the pattern also changed. Sana looked at Martha surprisingly she asked 'How did you do that?'

Martha laughed and said 'I can do anything....'

Sana was looking at Martha.

'After today's night everything will be changed' said Martha in a deep voice.

She was looking at Sana in a manipulative way. Sana was getting uncomfortable

'Why are you looking at me like this?' asked Sana.

'I am thinking how dumb you are; I thought you must be smart and challenging for me but you are such a dumb you made everything easy for me' said Martha.

'What do you mean Martha?' asked Sana with little anger and worry.

'If something happens to you between rituals; just imagine if you die then I will use your friends without any effort' said Martha.

Sana remained stunned after listening to this.

'you....u...know....ha...how' said Sana in a low voice and stumbling.

'Yes... I know Baby..... I know everything because I let you do that; you are just a key to open the door' said Martha in a manipulating way.

'no...you can't' said Sana

'Yes...I Can... I Did' said Martha.

Sana was feeling so guilty that she started crying, she wanted to stop them from coming here but she was not able to concentrate.

'You can't stop them Sana; you did that because I made you do that; now I don't want so you can't' said Martha laughing towards Sana.

Martha left the room and banged the door.

Sana sat on the bed. She was afraid and feeling guilty about what she had done.

'I have to do something....I have to do something... how can I stop them'

She closed her eyes and tried to concentrate and connect with Cam.

'Cam! Can you hear me?..... Cam please listen to me....don't come here it's a trap...Cam please'

But she was not able to connect with him. She didn't open her eyes as tears were running down her face. She was continuously thinking about Cam and suddenly she saw something....a visualization in her mind that all were in the car, Terry was driving and asking how far it was and Cam was there beside him.

Sana suddenly opened her eyes and thought "What was that? Was it true or just my imagination"

She closed her eyes again and started thinking about Cam, Blair, Sensei, and Herbert she saw Sensei was in headquarters and again the same car where Terry was driving cam was sitting next to him Blair and Herbert were sitting in the back seat with 2 unknown people.

She again opened her eyes and thought 'If it is real there must be a way to stop them; but how and what if it is also Martha's trap?....please somebody help me to stop them I want them to be safe...'

After a few seconds, Sana was feeling something weird something shiny and softly glittering waves were coming out from her skin. She was feeling warm when she saw her hand same waves were coming out from her palm. She tried to hold it together and those become stronger and warmer.

She spoke to herself 'What kind of energy is that? Why from my body? My skin?' that energy in her hand started floating in front of her she was looking at her and asked softly 'Can you help me to stop them?' and that energy suddenly went out from window at full speed. Sana kept looking at the window.

ꕥ

'We are half of our way' said Cam.

'great!' said Blair.

But suddenly something happened and the car stopped.

'What's wrong? Why did you stop the car Terry?' asked Blair.

'I don't know; something is wrong it's not starting' said Terry.

Everyone came out of the car Terry and Cam checked the engine 'Everything is looking fine then what happened?' asked Cam.

'I have no idea' said Terry. They again tried to start the car but nothing was happening.

'What happened Cam?' asked Herbert.

'Don't know everything is looking fine but not working' said Cam.

'Now what?' asked Shawn. 'That place is still 17 kilometres away' he continued

'We can use our ninja speed' said Daniel.

Everyone looked at him. 'We are not supposed to use it in front of other people' said Herbert.

'Yeah I know but right now we are in the middle of nowhere we can use it right now and when any town comes between we will speed down; easy, no one will understand' said Daniel.

'Well that makes sense I mean come on guys we used to do this before' said Shawn.

'Guys...I think I agree with both of them right now the most important thing is we need to find out Sana before moonrise' said Blair.

'Okay but if something happens you will be responsible' said Herbert pointing towards Daniel.

ෆ

It was 8 o clock in the morning Sana tried to do the same again she closed her eyes and started thinking about Cam, Blair, Herbert, and Terry and she saw everyone was walking through town for the West Coast

'They are walking it means that energy stopped their Car but what kind of energy was that? Oh! How can I forget about this pendant, it has different energy it doesn't look like that' Sana was talking to herself.

Suddenly Martha came in and banged the door with anger she asked 'What did you do?'

Sana was looking at her with little fear.

Martha grabbed her arm tightly and asked again with anger 'What did you do?'

'I don't understand what you are talking about' said Sana.

'You have done something.... tell me you bloody girl' said Martha banging her against the wall

'I did nothing please leave me... it's hurting' said Sana with pain.

Martha grabbed her face 'Look into my eyes' she shouted.

Sana looked into her eyes her eyes were moist because of pain but after looking into Sana's eyes Martha's face faded.

'No, It's not possible' Martha whispered.

'What?' asked Sana.

Martha lost her temper... and grabbed Sana's hair and banged her head on the wall harshly it was so hard that became unconscious and fell on the ground.

Martha looked at Sana and said 'I will be back.... just don't die

ꕤ

It was 9:30 AM and everyone reached at Koeberg nuclear power station.

'Don't you think we took a lot of time to reach here' said Shawn.

Everyone was unexpectedly tired... all of the breathing so heavy.

'Yah...I felt the same it was a very long road' said Cam 'Anyway we all are tired which is weird but you guys take a rest here I will ask some people if they have seen something weird' he continued.

'Okay!' said Herbert. And everyone nodded.

Cam asked many people if they had seen Sana by showing her photo and if they hadn't seen something weird happen but he didn't get any information.

He came back to the team after sometime

'Did you find something' asked Blair to Cam.

'No; I asked so many people but no one knows or noticed anything' said disappointed Cam.

'It's alright we will find her; do you have any idea in which exact area she was' asked Blair.

'She was in the middle of the ocean' said Cam.

'What are you kidding us in the middle of the ocean how are we going to find her look at the ocean nothing is there' said irritated Herbert.

'Herbert please control yourself, you are being rude' said Terry.

'Okay' said Herbert.

'Cam! Do you have anything that belongs to Sana?' asked Blair.

'Yeah; I have her earring' said Cam.

'Aww.. How romantic, you have her earring' said Daniel teasing Cam...

'No! I just found it on the ground in her apartment' said Cam.

'Oh! How careless!' said Shawn teasing Cam again.

'No! She is not careless at all; once I slapped her.... and that time her earring fell on the floor' said Cam.

'You slapped her? Are you serious?' said Daniel.

'Guys! Focus.... We can discuss it later' said Blair with little anger.

'Sorry' said Daniel and Shawn.

Blair took Sana's earring in her hand with some water took a deep breath and concentrate

after a few moments, she was able to feel something... she was quiet for some time.

'She is here somewhere; I can feel her presence' whispered Blair.

Everyone was looking at her

'Did you find her?' asked Cam.

'I am trying but I can't reach her' said Blair.

Blair sat down feeling low and said "I tried but some kind of energy is there trying to stop me; there are two different energies one tried to stop me and the other one tried to hurt me"

'Let me try I will try it through air' said Shawn.

'okay' said Blair.

Shawn took the earring and closed his eyes the wind got a little faster but the same happened with Shawn.

'Blair is right that second energy is trying to hurt but I sensed something' said Shawn.

'What?' asked Blair.

'Something is there in the ocean which we are not able to see. It's big and invisible but I don't know how far is that' said Shawn.

'If it is a big place it must be connected with the earth it's not floating; let me try I might find out how far is' said Daniel.

Daniel took the earring and put it on the ground (Earth) covered it with their hand and took a deep breath. He was silent for some time trying to sense every inch of the earth...

'It's not that far.... only one or one and a half kilometres far and the energy which is stopping us is Sana's energy she doesn't want us to find her' said Daniel.

'What? But Why?' asked Terry.

'I don't know; she is connected to earth right now she is on the ground and unconscious; Martha is trying to kill her energy that is why it hurting us' said Daniel.

'It means she is here but trying to hide herself; she is trying to protect us; and we have to do something differently so that we will find her without letting her know' said Cam.

'Cam she doesn't want us to find her, why don't you understand there is a danger' said Herbert.

'She is sacrificing her life for us; we can't let her die' said Cam.

'You are getting mad for her, you don't understand what you are doing; it's the end of her journey with us let her go' said Herbert.

'No I won't I will find her and save her' said Cam.

'You can't... no one of us knows where she is; she is hiding she is a coward' said Herbert.

'She is protecting us' shouted Cam.

'Here you go then let her protect us' said Herbert.

'No please; just help me to find her; just let me know where she is I will go on my own, you all will be safe' said Cam.

'She made you crazy; you are acting like her slave who is trying to save his master' said Herbert.

'Shut up Herbert! She did nothing, she is a pure soul' said Cam.

'Oh yes! How can I forget you owe her because she saved your life; but it doesn't mean you will let us die too' said Herbert.

'you are wrong Herbert...' said Cam.

'Then what is right tell me, why are you so desperate to save the girl who does not even matter in our life' said Herbert.

'She matters...She matters to me...' said Cam.

'Then why tell me...Why that bloody girl matters so much in your life' said Herbert.

'Herbert enough you are hurting him' said Blair.

'No! He has to tell us why is he risking his life to save her' said Herbert.

'Herbert enough...' said Blair.

'Tell me, Cam....' shouted Herbert.

'Because I love her.....' he said looking at Herbert.. his eyes were moist... 'She is innocent... please help me to find her... I am not able to do this alone... I need your help.....I am not ready to lose someone I love...It feels more than hell...I don't want that pain again......I am sorry I became selfish earlier but I don't even want to lose anyone of you' Cam sat down with tears in his eyes.

'Cam relax' said Blair rubbing his back and comforting him.

Herbert sat in front of Cam looked into his eyes and said 'If you love her then use your intelligence to that level and find the way hell out to find her. We all will help you' said Hervert and hugged Cam.

'Why are you so dramatic and manipulative' asked Cam.

Herbert chuckled and said 'Because it's me'

'I have a plan' said Cam.

'Tell us fast' said Shawn.

'We can use our powers together to find the exact place

'How?' asked Terry.

'Shawn you have air and fire element, Blair you have water and Daniel you have earth element so first you three will connect with the place together once you feel you reach there Herbert and Terry will make a structure on that invisible thing adding their power of thunder but make sure we don't want exact thunder we want it like thread lines and after that when we find the exact place I will freeze it and open the invisible way to enter

'Wow! That sounds great' said Daniel.

'Yes but it will take more energy' said Cam.

'No problem! Let's start it' said Shawn.

'No we have to wait until Sana becomes conscious' said Cam.

'Why?' asked Blair.

'Because we are using connection with Sana to find that place we need her to be conscious said Cam.

'Okay I will keep checking that; I will let you know if she moves' said Daniel.

'Okay, till then sit and take a rest' said Cam.

ꢁ

It was 6 PM

'I hope she is fine it's been too long we are waiting' said Blair.

'She is still at the same place' said Daniel.

After some time at 6:20

'Guys! She woke up she is moving' said Daniel.

'Great! Are you guys ready?' asked Cam.

'Yes' said everyone.

ꢁ

Sana woke up her head was hurting because of the injury.

She stood up and started looking everywhere she went near the window she realized the sun was getting down.

She smiled and said in her heart 'I don't know what energy you were but thank you for stopping them now they won't reach here, they will be safe...' and sat on the bed.

And again Martha entered the room and said "Come with me"

'Where?' asked Sana.

'I don't want any questions just come with me' said Martha.

Martha grabbed her hand and took her to another hall. The hall was very big and a little dark but full of candles and herbs and crystals. There was a small stage with a wooden pillar in the middle of the hall.

Martha grabbed Sana towards the wooden pillar and tied her with ropes. Sana looked upwards there was an open tomb and she was able to look at the sky.

Martha lightened up the candle with her magic she took some water from the big bowl and placed it in front of Sana.

And she started casting some spells.

ꟗ

Shawn, Blair, and Daniel found out about the invisible place, and Herbert and Terry were giving it shape.

'Guys fast moon is rising' said Blair

They heighten their energy to make it fast.

At 7 they found the exact place and Cam froze it and made the door to enter.

'Cam it's 7 you have only 22 minutes to find her' said Blair.

'And I am coming with you' said Terry.

'Brother!' said Herbert.

'I don't want any discussion about it Herbert I am going' said Terry.

'You don't have to' said Cam.

'She is my best friend too... I am coming' said Terry.

Cam nodded. Terry looked at Blair she smiled.

'Save her and come back' said Blair softly.

And they left.

At 7:10 they entered.

ꟗ

Martha was casting spells she stopped looked at Sana and smiled.

'What happened?' asked Sana.

'They are here' said Martha smiling like an evil.

'Who?' asked Sana.

Martha didn't say anything.

'Oh my god...Cam?' said Sana.

Martha smiled at started casting her spells again in a harsh way candles started glowing more and she started torturing Sana.

'Martha, what are you doing? It's hurting' said Sana in pain.

'You have to suffer more.....' said Martha

Started casting spells more powerfully

"et non dignum hac vita, sed et mori facias..... et non dignum hac vita, sed et mori facias..... et non dignum hac vita, sed et mori facias....."

Sana started screaming in pain

Cam and Terry heard Sana's scream

'Terry we need to go this way' said Cam.

And following her scream they reached the same hall.

.

'I was waiting for you said Martha while chanting her spells

'Leave her...' said Cam.

'Cam! Terry! You shouldn't be here...Gooo...Go back to school' shouted Sana.

'We are here to take you with us' said Terry.

'Nooo, Go please Go' Shouted Sana.

Cam and Terry attacked on Martha. But Martha was very powerful she shot them with her wand. Martha tied their hand and legs and hung them on the wall with her magic.

'Martha leave them...Please I beg you' said Sana crying.

'No honey I also need some fun right....well it's time to let them enjoy too' said Martha.

It was 7:20 PM and Martha started casting spells

"Hue lunae non ego sum servus tuus hic, ut diu ut serviamus tibi; nunc hoc puella ad sacrificium da mihi potestatem ego merear"

At 7:22 she took Sana's hand to take her blood she gave a deep cut to her hand and herself too and poured the blood into the bowl

"Ego tibi praecipio tibi u team in sanguine meo."

She adds all the blood in the big bowl filled with water in front of Sana. And let the reflection of the moon settle in the bowl.

She added all the herbs one by one and deep every crystal the color of water turned into dark green. Martha smiled she took a glass and took water and drink and told Sana to drink.

'I won't drink this blood' said Sana.

'You have to drink it' said Martha.

'Noo' said Sana.

'Drink it otherwise, I will kill your friend one by one' said Martha.

She pointed her wand at Terry and he started screaming in pain

'No..Don't I will drink' said Sana.

She drank all that water.

'That's like my good girl' said Martha and took down Terry's pain.

'Now the energy will come to you and you have to pass it to me okay?'

'I don't know how to do that' said Sana.

'The same way you stopped your friend' said Martha.

Moonlight getting sharper and something was happening with Sana. She was absorbing the energy very sharp energy. Her pendant got heated up.

'Now give me all energy you are absorbing' said Martha.

'I am trying but nothing is happening....' Said Sana.

'Do it otherwise, I will kill your other friend' shouted Martha.

She did the same with Cam. Cam was going through pain.

'Please don't I am trying' said Sana.

'You start I will stop' said Martha.

Sana looked at Cam he gestured to her that he trusted her and she could do anything.

Sana nodded and started sending her powers to Martha, it was a white aura.

Martha was laughing like an evil.

Sana was going through a lot of pain, it was unbearable

The process of transferring power was started Martha was becoming more powerful

Sana looked at Cam. He said softly "You can do it"

The supermoon was about to end in 10 minutes.

Sana used her all power and started absorbing all the power she was absorbing Martha's power too without letting her know.

But at one point Martha came to know what was happening

'You can't do this I will kill all your friends' shouted Martha.

'Yes, I can't because I already did that' said Sana.

Sana did not stop she continued absorbing her power. She was absorbing her orange aura also.

Martha was getting weaker.

“Stop it” Martha shouted.

‘I won’t’ said Sana speeding up

‘You will die’ said Martha.

‘I don’t care’ said Sana.

When Cam heard that he tried to stop Sana.

‘Sana stop!’ cam screamed

‘It’s too late Cam’ said Sana.

She pulled out Martha’s Soule from her body and at the same time crystal in Sana’s pendent broke. Sana broke all the ropes and she fell on the ground...... Cam and Terry were free from Martha’s magic.

They ran to Sana to wake her up

ꙮ

Sana and Martha’s souls entered the portal it was just a white none never-ending space.

‘You shouldn’t do that’ said Martha.

Sana looked into Martha’s eyes and said ‘You have to die Martha; I am not giving you any choice may your soul rest in peace’ said Sana.

‘You will regret’ said Martha and her soul became ash and disappeared.

What place is this? Sana was thinking.

‘Sana please help me’ she heard her voice.

Sana turned and was shocked. She saw herself dying.

‘who are you? You look like me; How?’ asked Sana.

‘I am you, Sana! From parallel universe’ said another Sana.

‘What?’ asked Sana.

‘She is right Sana’ one lady appeared in white formal Japanese wear.

‘Who are you? What is she saying? What place is this?’ asked Sana.

'Sana you are at one of the portals where many universes get connected that happened because of that stone in your pendent; that broke and a portal opened and your soul came here. Sana you have to help her; her universe needs your help they are going to be in more problems

'Am I dead?' asked Sana.

'Yes but temporarily' said the women.

'And what help do I have to do?' asked Sana.

'She is dying Sana. Her soul will disappear in a few moments. You have to take her place' said the woman.

'And what about my universe?' asked Sana.

'You will be there too' said Women.

'What?' Sana was surprised.

'Martha connected you with her body if she dies you will die too; you have to split your soul for two bodies' said Women.

'So what would I be? Dead or alive?' asked Sana.

'You will leave 2 lives at one time' said Women.

'What? How is it possible?' asked Sana.

'Martha was one of the strongest witch Sana and she is dead every witch get a chance to ask for one last wish before dying she connected you with another universe' said Women.

'And what if I don't want to go?' asked Sana.

'You have no choice, Sana. If you want to be alive then you have to live two lives and if you don't then you will never go back; this temporary death will become permanent.

'What? Are you serious?' asked Sana in worry.

'Yes Sana look at her Sana she has no time you have to make a decision faster' said Women.

'Okay I will help her' said Sana.

'Take her hand in your hand and say I accept you' said the woman.

'Sana went towards another Sana but the woman interrupted

'Before that let me tell you there will be some consequences she will not be that strong and she will forget everything and start a new life and whatever will happen to her will affect you and maybe you will have to go to another universe to help her but when you will go same will happen with you; you will lose the memory and complete her.'

'Okay' said Sana.

'Everything will be fine Sana I will be with you' said Women.

Sana took her hand and said I accept you.

Sana opened her eyes and saw her friend dead. She was shocked at screamed she closed her eyes tightly.

And she again opened her eyes with a choked throat as she tried hard to breathe. She found herself in Cam's arms. Cam was sitting on the floor holding Sana in his arms.

He became happy when Sana woke up. Happy tears were running out of his eyes and he couldn't stop smiling. he gave a tight hug to Sana. Sana couldn't stop smiling when she saw Cam.

Terry was happy to see both of them together.

They all went to the school and everyone welcomed Sana.

Sensei was very happy for everyone. Sana stayed under the observation of doctors for 2 days and then the school celebrated the victory.

Sana went to Sensei

Sensei smiled and said 'I am proud of you Sana, now get ready your new life has been started'

IX

I am...

'Hey!' said Daniel.

Sana turned back she saw Daniel standing behind her and said with a smile 'Hey! You must be Daniel; Am I right?'

Daniel chuckled 'Yes'

'Great! Cam told me about you yesterday; thank you so much for helping Cam to find me' said Sana.

'Oh please, No problem; so how's your health now? And did you learn about your powers?' asked Daniel.

'I am absolutely fine I am feeling stronger than before, and about powers, I haven't learned anything yet I don't know how to use them and am not able to control them you know...' said Sana.

'yeah... I understand...umm... well I wanted to ask you something' said Daniel.

'Sure!' replied Sana.

'Are you in transition?' asked Daniel with concern.

'I don't understand what are you talking about... What transition?' said Sana.

'Are you becoming a Vampire?' whispered Daniel.

'What? Noo...' said Sana with surprise.

'Are you sure?' asked Daniel.

'Yes...First of all, they don't exist but I don't know if whatever happening nowadays though if they do exist I never see one... But why are you thinking like this?' said Sana.

'Because Martha forced you to drink her blood and you did that and after some time you died' said Daniel.

Sana was looking at him in shock and asked him 'Wait...What you just said? I died...'

'Yes! And you came back after 9 minutes that is really very weird' said Daniel.

'How do you know that I was dead and who else knows that?' asked Sana.

'Because I was connected with you...I mean when we were finding you Cam gave me your earring and we found you throw that but I had that earring till the end till you came back so I sensed that' said Daniel.

'And who else knows that?' asked Sana.

'No one; just me' said Daniel.

'Look, Daniel, yes I died but it was temporary; my soul went somewhere else and it was a kind of portal but after some time I came back' said Sana.

'And what happened there?' asked Daniel.

'I don't remember everything; when I came back my brain was frying and whatever I remember is just one thing that lady, she told me that Martha has done something terrible and I am going to face some consequences' said Sana.

'What consequences?' asked Daniel.

'I have no idea' said Sana.

'Okay... everything will be fine' said Daniel smiling.

'Yes! And one more thing Martha was a witch, not a Vampire, so I am not in a transition' said Sana chuckling trying to lighten the environment

ꙮ

'Hey! Why are you not talking with me?' asked Terry.

Sana looked At Terry and said 'Because I don't know you... I don't talk with strangers'

'Sana! I am your best friend, not a stranger' said Terry.

'No, you are a spy' said Sana.

'What happened? Why are you so mad at him?' asked Blair.

'Because he pretended to be my best friend, he was actually babysitting me for three months' said Sana madder at Terry.

'Sana you have misunderstanding' said Terry convincing Sana.

'Sana, Sansei told me to look after you that's why I didn't tell you that I am a part of this school' said Terry.

'Oh that's the reason you didn't tell us about your secret work' said Shawn.

Terry nodded.

'Sooo...' Sana was about to say something but Terry interrupted 'Don't say anything first listen to me'

Sana stopped

'Sensei told me to look after you but he didn't tell me to be your friend it was all my choice and also we didn't become your friend because I wanted to be it just happened with time. Yes, I agree that I did not tell you about this school and you have all right to be mad at me about it but except for this thing everything was true' said Terry.

'Okay...So...give me proof that you are not lying right now' said Sana narrowing her eyes.

'Remember I told you about the blond girl?' Terry whispered in her ears.

Sana looked at him thinking about it, she narrowed her eyes again, 'Blond girl...'

She looked At Blair and raised her eyebrows with surprise.

'Is that Blair?' asked Sana with surprise.

Terry nodded with a soft smile.

'Oh my god...OMG....OMG...Woow.....' Sana was very happy; she was excited like a kid.

'It means you both are dating' said Sana with excitement.

Blair blushed.

Sana was so happy and she hugged both of them together. But she realized that she had become overexcited she stepped back and said 'I am sorry, I just got overexcited' with an embarrassed smiley face.

Terry and Blair started laughing and they both hugged her back.

'So! Now you are not mad at me right?' asked Terry.

'No... as per our rules if you want forgiveness I am going to tell one of you a secret' said Sana with a mischievous smile.

'That is going to be fun' said Daniel.

'So, when we were in Worcester Terry used to flirt with Mrs. Oliver' said Sana.

Everyone looked at Terry with narrow eyes.

'What? She was a cute old lady' said Terry defending him.

Everyone was staring at him and then busted with laughter.

'Did I miss something?' asked Cam coming towards everyone.

'Your girl is so funny' slipped out of Daniels's mouth.

'What?' asked Sana looking at Daniel.

'I guess my tongue is twisting a lot and I am feeling thirsty, I am going to grab some juice' said Daniel and left the place.

'Where were you?' asked Sana.

'Sensei called Herbert and me for some work so we were there' said Cam.

'Okay' said Sana.

There was an awkward silence for some moments.

'So are you enjoying?' asked Cam.

'Yah...I came to know many interesting things' said Sana.

'Great... what are those things?' asked Cam.

'That Terry and Herbert are siblings and Blair and Terry are dating' said Sana.

'You didn't know about it?' asked Cam.

'Nope' replied Sana. 'But they look really cute together' she continued.

'Yeah...' said Cam Looking at Sana.

***

In another universe, Sana opened her eyes in the hospital after one week.

Sana opened her eyes and she found herself lying on the bed, her hands full of Saline and other types of equipment. Monitors around her bed were beeping continuously. She was looking here and there to watch someone and one lady came to her and said 'Hello girl!'

The doctor came in and started checking her

'Are you able to breathe normally?' asked the doctor.

Sana nodded.

He looked into her eyes with a torch.

'Can you move your eyes without pain?' asked Doctor.

She looked everywhere without turning her neck.

'Okay; good you are out of danger girl' said the doctor.

But Sana was looking at the doctor silently.

'Now tell me everything your name and what happened to you' said Doctor.

Sana was just kept staring at the wall.

'We are doctors you can trust us; we need to know everything only then we will be able to treat you correctly' said Doctor.

'I am Anika, and I was driving home from the party and I met with an accident' said Sana.

'Do you remember everything? Who is that lady?' asked Doctor.

'Yes I do remember everything, she is my legal guardian Stella Motogami' said Anika.

'And who are your parents? Where are they?' asked Doctor.

'I never saw them...I was in the orphanage since I was kid ... and she has been my guardian since I was 17' said Anika.

ꕥ

'How are you feeling Anika?' asked Stella.

'I am fine Stella it's just my head is feeling empty' said Anika.

Stella nodded 'We will go home after a few days, you will be fine soon'

Anika nodded.

ꕥ

'Please help me, Sana! Please help me...It's hurting... I can't live like this... you have to come, Sana... A girl was lying on the ground and she was in extreme pain... Sana wanted to help her but she got stuck she felt the invisible glass between them and she was not able to move... Some people came in and started dragging that girl... Noo...Stop don't hurt her Stop..Sana was screaming... Sana looked at them in anger and waved her hands towards them and fire appeared.......Sana open your eyes someone shouted. my eyes are open she replied...Sana open your eyes...'

Sana opened her eyes and she found her bed on fire and Blair was shouting her name.

Blair took some water in her hand sprinkled everywhere and waved her hands, and water covered Sana's bed like a shower for a few seconds and the fire was contained after that.

Blair took Sana out of her bed.

'Are you okay?' asked Blair.

Sana was in shock she said 'I am fine Blair but how did this happen?'

'I have no idea, Sana, You were screaming in sleep, and when I came to see you suddenly the bed caught fire' said Blair.

'What?' said shocked Sana.

Sana remembered her dream and she was stunned. She took the support of the wall to stand and became worried.

'Sana, what happened? Are you okay' asked worried Blair.

'That fire... I did that...in my dreams' said worried Sana.

'Oh my god' replied Blair.

ဢ

Sana was taking a slow walk on the grass in the morning and Cam was running on the track. He saw Sana and noticed that she was in deep thought.

'Hey good morning' said Cam.

Sana looked up and saw Cam and said 'Hey Cam! Good morning'

Cam looked at Sana and said 'Why are you looking so tired? Are you okay?'

'Yeah I am fine but I am worried about my powers, I am not able to control them and not even able to understand them' said Sana.

'Don't worry we are trying to fix it, we will come to know what powers you have' said Cam

'Yeah but I think we need to hurry because something happened yesterday night' said Sana.

Cam stopped walking and asked 'What happened?'

Sana took a deep breath and said 'I woke up with fire on my bed'

Cam was shocked 'What? How did that happen?'

'It happened because of me I did something in my dream and that happened in reality' said Sana.

'I think we need to find the solution ASAP' said Cam with a serious note.

ꙮ

'Stella, Can I ask you something?' said Anika.

Stella looked at her and said 'Sure!'

'Something is weird' said Anika.

Stella narrowed her eyes and asked 'What weird?'

'It's been two weeks since I got discharged from the hospital and there are some things I am not able to understand' said Anika.

'Will you explain what exactly happening?' asked Stella.

'It feels like I know everything but I don't remember anything about it' said Sana with confusion.

'What do you mean?' asked Stella.

'I mean, look... the phone you are using, I know which company is this, what function it has, I know everything about its camera, internal memory, processor everything... but I don't remember if I have ever used it or not, if I have ever used it I don't remember when; and if I didn't then how do I know everything about it and I don't even remember if I have ever read about it' said Anika with concern. She continued 'And it is not only about devices it is about everything people, place, and information everything.'

Stella walked towards Anika with deep thinking she sat beside her and said 'Anika I do understand what is happening but we will talk about it later you need rest, now you just relax I will give you the head massage you will feel better'

Anika nodded and she lay on the bed. She put both of her hands on Anika's head, looked into her eyes, and said 'You went through a very big accident so you lost some part of your memory and you are not going to discuss it with anyone do you understand? now you should sleep' and she pressed her fingers on Anika's head.

Anika became cold for a second and again became normal.

'Stella I think I should sleep' said Anika.

'Sure!' replied Stella.

ꙮ

At the same time when Sana and Cam were talking with each other...

Sana's head suddenly started to hurt a lot. She grabbed her head and cried out with pain.

'Sana, what is happening to you?' asked Cam holding her.

'I don't know... my head... Cam, it's hurting a lot' said Sana in pain.

Cam took her to the bench and told her to sit down and gave her water to drink.

But she can't.

'Cam it's frying... my brain is frying...' said Sana.

After a few moments that stopped and Sana became normal. She opened her eyes and took a deep breath. Cam gave her water to drink.

'Are you feeling okay?' asked Cam.

'Yeah, I am fine' replied Sana. She stood up and looked around and said 'But what are we doing here?'

Cam was looking at her with a confused face. He asked 'What are you talking about?'

'How did I come here? Cam what time is it?' asked Sana in confusion.

'Sana, it's almost 6 AM' said Cam looking at Sana.

'What? How is this possible?' said Shocked Sana.

'Sana we've been talking for the last 10 minutes and I don't understand what is happening right now' said Cam.

'I think something is wrong with my mind, I don't remember anything since yesterday evening' said Sana.

'It doesn't sound good' said Cam looking at Sana in worry.

To be continued...

www.ingramcontent.com/pod-product-compliance
Lightning Source LLC
LaVergne TN
LVHW041046150826
845672LV00001B/486

* 9 7 9 8 8 9 1 8 6 1 5 1 0 *